The Surveillance
Tales of White Terror in Taiwan

C. J. Anderson-Wu

To my very supportive family

To Mr. Yang Ching-Chu / 楊青矗
The writer I respect greatly
Many of my fictional works are inspired
by his life stories

Table of Content

The Friend in the Remote South

Summer 1972, Kaohsiung, Taiwan

Yang San-Jih liked to go to the library on Sundays. He made very little money at the refinery, and he had no girlfriend to date, so the library was the most practical place to spend his time. It was a four-floor building, quiet with very few people. On the first floor was the lobby with the check-out counter and a children's reading room. On the second floor were bookshelves of science, health, history, religion, music, and arts. On the third floor were bookshelves of psychology, philosophy, home economics, language studies, Chinese literature and foreign literature. The public was not allowed to enter the fourth floor where the offices of the library administration were located.

The bookshelves of each category consisted of very few books, so medical books were merged into the category of health, and geography into history. Even with those additions, the library's collection for each subject was still far from adequate. Still, Yang San-Jih took out books with titles that aroused his curiosity, and tried to find enough to continue reading. Of course he couldn't understand a lot of them, like astronomy which was very abstract to him. And philosophy seemed like riddles. He liked reading more about history, religion, and literature. He found translated fiction particularly interesting. Since he had discovered it, he had read Fyodor Dostoevsky, Franz Kafka, and John Steinbeck. Yang San-Jih had never heard of these writers before, and he didn't understand all of their works even after reading them from cover to cover. But that never dampened his curiosity about these stories created a long time ago and far away.

Today he noticed that there were several books on a smaller desk beside the counter with a sign that said "New Releases." He walked toward them and saw that there were some detective novels by South African writers. He had never heard of "detective novels," so he took one and started reading it. It was about a retired police officer who worked as a private detective and was commissioned to find a young woman who had been either abducted or seduced away from her rich parents. A librarian walked by and told him, "You can check it out if you like."

So Yang San-Jih brought this book, *The Missing Woman,* back home and read it in his dorm. He read it carefully so as not to overlook any clues about the missing woman's whereabouts. Of course in the end he did not correctly guess what had actually happened to the woman, but it was fun to read a detective novel.

Da! As he was absorbed by the novel, one of his roommates snapped his fingers and surprised him. "What are you reading?" Yang San-Jih showed his roommate the cover of the novel.

"What is it about?"

"I've finished reading it, you can have it if you want to read it. But you will have to return it to the library by the end of next weekend."

"I can't read. Tell me the story."

"What do you mean you can't read?"

"I am illiterate."

"How come you are illiterate? Everyone attends

school for at least six years."

"I did, but I have a problem reading."

Yang San-Jih tried to respond but did not know what to say. He too had taken only the mandatory elementary school education, but it never stopped him from learning. On the other hand, there were many people who had to support their families at a young age and couldn't attend school regularly. And this guy, a temp mover, unemployed from time to time, was hardly a self-learner. He considered how he might tell his roommate about the detective story he had just read, but it was difficult. How do you retell a story from a book? He flipped the pages of the book and thought perhaps he should read it again before the deadline of the return date and think about how to tell this story orally. But his roommate had already set his mind on other things, and no longer seemed to be curious about the story.

In the dining room of the refinery, as Yang San-Jih was reading during his meal, he attracted another co-worker's attention. "What are you reading, San-Jih?" It was Kao Heh-Shun, a junior engineer about Yang San-Jih's age. He showed Kao Heh-Shun the book cover.

"Um, interesting." Kao took the book and looked it over carefully.

"There is still about a week before the return date. If you are interested you can have it for the week." Usually an engineer like Kao Heh-Shun wouldn't have any interaction with a janitor like Yang San-Jih. Not only were their tasks and workplaces different but also they held different levels of stature in the company. Kao's inquiry made Yang San-Jih feel like his stature was being elevated.

But Kao put the book back on the table, beside Yang San-Jih's tray of food. "Do you know why these kinds of books are published?"

Yang San-Jih was confused by Kao Heh-Shun's question. He never thought about why a book was written or published. He had seen that there were a lot of books in the library containing great knowledge, and novels by authors with big names containing wise thoughts. And this detective novel was fun to read. Was the answer that they brought money to the publishers?

"This is not even an original work. It is a second-class imitation of Raymond Chandler."

"What?"

"Raymond Chandler, an American mystery novelist."

"Oh. I never heard of him."

"But that's not the point. Come to my dorm after work; we can talk about it. And I have books you might find interesting."

Hearing about Kao Heh-Shun's books, Yang San-Jih's face brightened. He replied immediately, "Sure. See you after work." He felt excited that an engineer had invited him to talk about books.

Yang San-Jih looked back at his detective novel, trying to remember the name of the American mystery and crime writer. He thought to himself, "I've got to ask Kao Heh-Shun again tonight." Excited, he left the diner for his afternoon tasks in a hurry without finishing his lunch. He figured that the sooner his work was done, the quicker he could go to meet with Kao.

Kao Heh-Shun's dormitory was actually the same style as Yang San-Jih's, only Yang San-Jih was sharing it with three other men, and Kao had it all to himself. There was a small refrigerator, and a couch sat where the bunk bed would have been in Yang San-Jih's dorm. There were bookshelves between the windows.

Kao Heh-Shun took out several books from a self-made drawer at the bottom of a bookshelf and showed them to Yang San-Jih, "These are the real literature of South Africa."

Yang took them and looked them over, amazed by the covers with languages he did not know and photos of authors, some of them with really dark skin. Nevertheless, it felt good to touch the pages. He opened them and enjoyed the unique smell of books.

"What languages are these?"

"English and Afrikaan." Kao Heh-Shun grabbed a couple more books and demonstrated the contents to Yang San-Jih.

"Neither of them I know." Yang San-Jih said regretfully.

"I don't know Afrikaan either, and even my English reading needs the help of a dictionary from time to time." Kao Heh-Shun said politely, knowing Yang's eagerness to know what was to be found in those publications. He added, "I am thinking of organizing a group of friends to translate them into Chinese so we can share these works with more readers." Yang San-Jih was happy to know that one day he might read them in translation.

"But of course I invited you to come not to show off my collection of south African literature." He moved two chairs for them to sit down and talk. "Most of the outstanding South African writers are either in jail or in exile. Their works are banned in their country. These books are published by British or American publishing houses."

"Why?" Yang was stunned. Writers in jail or exiled? What could they have done?

"They are activists against apartheid, and they write about it."

"What's apartheid?"

"Separating black people from white people.

Repressing black people's rights, and limiting social resources available to black people."

"Oh. I see." Yang remembered several months ago he had seen on the TV news that the South African president was a white man.

"Because of the apartheid, South Africa is boycotted or sanctioned by many countries, so Taiwan became one of its few trade partners."

"What's boycott? What's sanction?"

"Not to have any trade with them." Kao explained, "It causes great damage to their economy, pressing the government to stop apartheid."

"I see. But Taiwan is still doing business with South Africa?"

"Yes. Because we don't have many friends, either. Ever since our seat in the United Nations was replaced by China, South Africa became a remote but close friend of Taiwan."

"It means, officially we are not against apartheid," Yang concluded, not without remorse.

"Correct. Our government pretends not to see it in order to maintain its very rare friendship in international society. Last year the two countries signed an agreement to enhance their partnership, and a cultural exchange was one of their cooperative endeavors. That's why all the public libraries in Taiwan have begun to have fiction translated from South African books."

"Oh, I see. And they publish our books, too?"

"Yeah, those shit writings." Kao Heh-Shun said in a very contemptuous tone, "Both countries have very oppressive censorship, so how can anyone expect that they would publish great literature?"

"What is censorship?" Yang San-Jih continued to raise questions about terms he had never heard of. He was confident that Kao Heh-Shun wouldn't make fun of his ignorance.

"It's when people in power check on everything

that is written or spoken. And if they find anything violating their authority, the writers and the speakers are in trouble."

"But how can they check on everything people write and say? We write and say so much every day."

"Any publication has to apply for a permit before publishing, and the same with any public gathering."

Oh, so all the books he saw in the library had been checked and permitted? The books about hydraulics, or photography, or even cooking, were all checked first?

"Not all books have the power to shake up the authority, but literature is the number one enemy of the ruling class." Kao seemed to see through what Yang San-Jih was thinking, "We have quite a few excellent literary works about anti-colonialism during the Japanese colonial time, but you can guess that the South African regime doesn't like anti-colonialism at all. So they only picked up some mediocre stories, poems and essays that tell you how to be a good man, how beautiful nature is, and other clichés."

"We have banned books, too?"

"Of course. A lot of them. Books on leftist thinking, like socialism or Marxism, were certainly banned. Essays criticizing the ruling party were also banned. Anthologies campaigning for direct democracy had to be banned. Books that law enforcement defined as obscene also had to be banned. Naturally their definition of obscenity was wide open and could be used to ban anything in print."

"The government bans books, and puts writers in jail? Isn't that too harsh of an environment for writers?"

"It is. But it's more complicated than that. First, these writers are mostly activists, too. They are persecuted by the state with all kinds of charges, like being communists, committing espionage, or agitating to cause riots. Second, putting writers behind bars can intimidate others who plan to write something unfavored by the authority." Kao Heh-Shun explained his points calmly, but then added in barely-restrained anger, "In this respect, Taiwan and South Africa are really buddies."

Yang San-Jih glanced at the covers of those South African books again. Now he wished he could read them immediately. "Tell me, tell me what you know about these authors."

Kao Heh-Shun picked up one of the books with a drawing of a dark-skinned boy on the cover, saying, "This book, *When Rain Clouds Gather,* is written by a young woman, Bessie Head. Her mother was a white woman, and her father was her mother's family servant. You can imagine that their union would be taboo in South Africa. They said her mother had a mental illness, and that was why she slept with a black man and bore his child. Who knows? When a person's behavior is deemed indecent by her society, there will be all kinds of rumors, not to explain the possible causes, but to provide comfort that there must be reasons for things beyond their understanding or tolerance.

"Anyway, Bessie escaped South Africa in 1964 because of her involvement with the activities against the colonial government. Her works are published by publishers in New York or London."

Kao Heh-Shun stood up to find iced water from the refrigerator for himself and Yang before continuing his introduction of his collection. "This man, Breyten Breytenbach, had to run to Paris because he married a Vietnamese French woman. It's illegal for white South Africans to have interracial marriages."

"White people must marry white people?"

"Exactly." Kao Heh-Shun nodded, and added, "Of course this is not the only trouble for Breyten Breytenbach. He opposes apartheid actively, and the government accuses him of being a terrorist."

"But he is a white man…"

"Yes, many white people are activists against apartheid. The struggle for black people's rights can't be fought by black people only. They are too oppressed."

Yang San-Jih was very agitated. Those people had taken risks to earn rights for themselves and for others. He was realizing that what he learned tonight was much more than what he could learn from the news media, or even from the library. "How do you know all about these issues? And how do you have these books?" He asked Kao Heh-Shun.

"We have a reading club." Kao Heh-Shun said carefully. Then, after a moment of considering, he said, "If you are interested, you can join us."

Reading clubs turned out to be a big issue in Taiwan throughout the period of Martial Law. People found writing, publishing, reading, or sharing banned publications would be indicted. Led by Kao Heh-Shun in the secret gatherings for book readings, Yang San-Jih absorbed knowledge at a speed beyond what he could have had imagined before. The more he knew, the more he realized how necessary such kinds of secret activities were, and why they were prohibited by the government. His anger towards the regime increased as his understanding of it accumulated, and the more he learned from his pals through their knowledge sharing, the more danger he could sense in their activities. Of course they took actions, individually and together. For Yang San-Jih, trying to write down his thoughts on social inequality, untransparent policy-making, and the autonomy of Taiwanese society among other issues to disturb authority was what he had been doing ever since, and he certainly got himself in trouble with the ruling class. But Yang San-Jih never backed down. The more he wrote, the more he felt the power of literature.

About fifteen years later, after writing and editing several books banned by the government, spending four years in jail as a political dissident, and finally getting his name cleared, Yang San-Jih was sent to the Iowa Writers' Workshop by the government to represent Taiwanese literature. Through an interpreter he interviewed one of his fellow writers in the Workshop, a young and furious South African writer, Hein Willemse, who just published his book of poetry *Angsland* in Afrikaans. Yang San-Jih raised several questions, whose answers he himself knew better than anyone.

How could politics affect the development of literature? How does a writer broaden his perspective and themes while focusing on the matters about which he is committed to making a difference?

Three decades later, the 78 year-old Yang San-Jih was reconnected with Hein Willemse via email, who became a professor of linguistics in South Africa after the abolition of apartheid. Not until then did Prof. Willemse know that Yang was a former political prisoner when they met in Iowa.

How would his old friend respond now to the same questions Yang Shan-Jih had raised three decades ago?

kô lat ons march for: freedom isn't free. verstaan djy pêllie? *
(come let's march for: freedom isn't free. d'you understand, pal?)

Yang San-Jih is really happy that his old friend in the remote south is still rebellious as he is.

Hein Willemse, "fokkie dice pêllie" (fuck d' dice ol' pal), Angsland, 1981

The Tax Collector

As Chiang Sung-Nien walked toward the office, he heard the telephone ringing crazily. He suspected it was his phone, and his colleagues were just letting it ring. He rushed through the doorway and picked up the receiver as quickly as he could. The caller's shrill voice hurt his ears, "You are asked to report to Consultant Chang as soon as possible!"

"Who?"

"Is this Chiang Sung-Nien?"

"Yes."

"Then you are asked to report to Consultant Chang immediately."

"Who is Consultant Chang?"

"Consultant Chang Hsien-Chung from the Domestic Security Office."

"There is a Domestic Security Office in our company?"

"Idiot, Domestic Security Office of the Investigation Bureau!" The caller hung up the phone without even identifying himself, leaving Chiang in a fog. Why was he asked to report to the Investigation Bureau today? Was he in trouble? He went to the rows of cabinets and dug out a handbook of all the telephone numbers of governmental organizations.

"Is this the Investigation Bureau?"

"Who is speaking?"

"This is… uh… I am asked to report to the Domestic Security Office. My name is Chiang Sung-Nien."

"How do you write your name?"

"Chiang as a sheep over a woman, Sung is like a pine tree, Nien is like the year."

"Where are you calling from?"

"Sino Petroleum… the Second Personnel Office."

"OK, I've taken note of it. The Domestic Security Office may call you back."

The whole morning Chiang was on pins and needles, wondering what he had done wrong. He couldn't concentrate on work, and after two hours of trying to busy himself, waiting for the phone call from the Investigation Bureau, he decided to go to the restroom first, then check his previous work in case he had made mistakes that he was still unaware of.

He opened the carbon copy of the report he had written earlier in the week:

> *After the U.S. announced that it was rec-ognizing the People's Republic of China and cutting off its official ties with the Republic of China (Free China, or the democratic island of Taiwan), these anti-reunionists planned a congregation in order to make a statement and respond to the US announcement. What they were going to state is still not clear, but they had already had several small gatherings during the preceding weeks. Attendees included Huang Hsin-Chieh, Yu Deng-Fa, Shih Ming-*

Chiang wondered if his report wasn't comprehensive enough. He had learned to withhold excessive information from the weekly report for the time when he found nothing and had nothing to write. That way his reports would look like he had valuable findings every week.

Perhaps he should add that he saw Yang San-Jih visit a woman working in the textile company several times over the past weeks. Was Yang having an affair with this woman? She was in her early thirties, plump, always wearing cheap, poorly-fitted skirt suits. She wasn't attractive at all, Chiang couldn't imagine that Yang would be involved with this woman. Chiang had no desire to conduct an investigation of extramarital affairs, which he did not think had anything to do with national security, and he wasn't interested in spying on the unattractive woman. He knew some of his colleagues liked that kind of shit, and they justified their gossip-chasing by making up connections with communist conspiracies or other ridiculous plots. But perhaps he should go ahead and add Yang's meetings with the woman, so that when his bosses from the

Bureau criticized him, he would have something to make up. He was still convinced, however, that this woman couldn't have anything to do with communist scheming. She was too homely to be a seducer.

Chiang looked up at his colleagues. Everyone's head was bent down, but he was very clear that they were just pretending to be engaged in work; a lot of times he had to do the same thing. Each of them was assigned to watch three to five people working for the Sino Petroleum Company, and at least one of them must be guilty or suspicious of something. So their watchers would devote time and energy to following them, not so much as to prevent crimes, but to fill their weekly reports. The more immoral things they could find, the easier it was for them to write their reports.

Chiang shared this office with four other men. The working title for each of them was "clerk", a most ambiguous word for their ambiguous missions. If they were promoted by the Bureau, they might be called "specialists," without clarifying what their specialty was, and given a small raise. Although they were supposed to conduct surveillance, they never were appropriately trained to be professional surveillers. Were they investigators or agents? They did not have any investigating skills or tools. They just followed people, and a lot of times the people they watched knew they were being watched. Was Yang aware he was being watched? Sometimes Chiang felt Yang certainly was, but sometimes he wasn't so sure. The acknowledgement of being watched would change everything, and it would translate into failure for Chiang in his work. Thus the only way out for Chiang was to assume that Yang had no idea that he was being watched.

The office was bleak today. A gloomy day in February. The grey iron shelves and cabinets did not reflect much of the weak light from the windows. Piles of old reports were everywhere, catching nothing but dust. He and his colleagues were supposed to be responsible for monitoring the national loyalty of the nearly two hundred employees of the Sino Petroleum Company, which was an unlikely task for five untrained men.

Chiang stood up, thinking perhaps he should dust the cabinets on his right hand side while he was waiting. Then the phone rang.

"Yes?"

"Is this Chiang Sung-Nien?"

"Yes."

"Hold on," The phone was transferred to another person in the Domestic National Security Office.

"Yes, sir?"

"Did you read the short story written by Yang San-Jih?"

"No. What short story?"

" 'The Tax Collector,' published by the Independent Daily today."

Chiang began to sweat. He had noticed that Yang wrote a lot. He carried his pen and notebook with him all the time, and scribbled from time to time. But Chiang had no idea that Yang was writing stories and had been published by the newspaper.

"This story has seriously damaged the image of the government!" Consultant Chang shouted at the other end of the telephone. He demanded that Chiang check it out and present a report about it.

Chiang rushed to the reading room and found that day's copy of the Independent Daily. In the supplement, Yan San-Jih's story covered two thirds of the page. Chiang sat down and read it carefully. It was about a female accountant of a small electronic business who was in charge of reporting the taxes of the business every two months. As it happened, it was a common practice for all businesses in Taiwan to have two accounting reports, a "secret accounting sheet" and an "official accounting sheet". The secret sheet was for the business owners to have a record of how much money they really had made and spent, and the official sheet was for taxation. They would hide their actual profit and exaggerate their expenses so they could pay less taxes.

In Yang's story, the accountant, Wan-Ching, was asked by her boss to evade as much taxes as possible. The business grew fast. It expanded from a small shop repairing electronic components into a busy manufacturing business. The commodity tax from sales was the easiest to evade, so Wan-Ching reduced the revenue from their sales to almost half of the actual number. Because of her capacity to save so much money for the company, she had been promoted and given raises several times. Her boss always said, "If all businesses in Taiwan reported taxes honestly, eight out of ten businesses would go bankrupt."

Wan-Ching learned that she needed to bribe the tax collectors when she turned the reports and invoices in to the tax office the first week of every odd month. The tax collector would pick out unmatched numbers or unusual expenditures, such as the silk quilt her boss bought, which should not have been considered a company procurement, "Why does an electronic component factory need a silk quilt?" The tax collector asked grimly. Wan-Ching knew if he kept looking, he'd find that all of her boss's household expenditures were reported as company costs, from his new TV to his son's shoes, from his wife's purse to his daughter's Hong Kong holiday trip.

Reading this, Chiang Sung-Nien couldn't help but laugh. It was very common in Taiwan for a business owner to consider the business to be his own personal possession and to have the business pay for everything for him and his family. No matter how hard his employees worked, the business wouldn't make any profit because the more the workers produced, the more their employer and his family could spend. The owner's family would move to a bigger house, drive fancier cars, and take more frequent vacations.

Chiang Sun-Nien read on. Wan-Ching got the address of the tax collector, and in the night she brought him a box of pears with bills of five thousand Taiwan dollars under the pears. By the next morning her company was notified that the tax report was okay.

That's the part that the Domestic Security Office worries might damage the governmental image, Chiang Sung-Nien told himself. Who doesn't know that tax evasion is the reality of every industry of Taiwan, or that bribery of tax collectors is common practice for every business? Chiang thought, with a mocking smile. If the government thinks this practice tarnishes the governmental image, then the action needed is an investigation of the tax offices of every city, every county, and every township, not an order for Chiang to write a report about a published short story.

Chiang Sung-Nien was intrigued by the story; he wondered how Yang San-Jih would come up with an ending. The story went on to say that Wan-Ching had to deal with different tax collectors after the Chinese New Year holiday. One of them refused to take any bribery from Wan-Ching. The other, although he also expressed a reluctance toward bribery, started asking Wan-Ching out, until Wan-Ching became sick of dating a man who didn't interest her at all. The one honest tax collector ended up costing her company a lot of money—the taxes they were supposed to pay, plus a high amount of fines. And the other one cost Wan-Ching a lot of time and energy taken from her personal life. In the end, Wan-Ching quit her job as a well-paid accounting chief of the electronic factory, and she started working at the assembly line of another factory. She made much less money, but felt much less burdened.

Chiang Sung-Nien got to his feet and considered how he was going to write the report. He did not think the story would have any impact on the government's image. And even it did, it should not be Yang's or his responsibility. Unfortunately, there was no way for him to argue with his superiors. He'd complete his report anyway.

****

Yang San-Jih was very happy that his first short story has been published by the Independent Daily. He had submitted the story "The Tax Collector" six weeks ago, and the editor had replied to his submission the following week, telling him that his work had been read and congratulating him on its publishing. Nevertheless, considering there were many excellent works, normally an accepted article wouldn't be published until four to eight weeks after its acceptance. The editorial desk would mail the author the pages of the article after it was published, but they couldn't tell them the exact day it would appear in publication.

After he got the letter, Yang San-Jih began to check the supplement of the Independent Daily everyday, hoping and wondering if he would be lucky enough to get his article published earlier than expected. After one and a half months, he finally saw it in the newspaper. He was so thrilled. It was his first story and first submission ever, and he had spent a lot of time and energy on it. Now he felt he was really a writer, which meant so much to him.

Yang San-Jih had had very little education. He had to drop out of high school when his father was killed by an accident at the construction site where he worked. At first he took odd jobs here and there to support his mother and siblings. Then he got the job as a janitor for the refinery of the Sino Petroleum in Kaohsiung. He lived in the dormitory with other low-ranking employees of the company, and his only hobby was reading. Every weekend he went to the municipal library to check out books. He devoured the knowledge contained in the books. He read in the night after work, in the early morning before going to work, and anytime he could manage to take his book out and flip through the pages. He hated to put down a book, so he even read when having meals or between tasks at work. He read faster and faster and became curious about everything.

It was when he learned that his cousin had to buy off government employees in the tax office of his hometown to maintain silence about cheating on their tax reports that he began to think the only way to disclose such immoral behavior was to make the real situation into a fictional creation. He was especially impressed by a book titled *Literature as Resistance,* an anthology that showed how literary works could wake up readers regarding incidents or issues they were not aware of, or had never cared about. One essay asserted that literature represents the struggles of the helpless and the hopeless, and if they are to achieve any success in solving their problems, literary works provide the only path to liberation. This essay used several examples, most of which Yang did not understand, but some sentences from one poem in particular stayed in his head all the time. It was written by an American poet Mark Strand and titled "Breath."

when you see them
tell them I am still here
that I stand on one leg while the other one dreams
that this is the only way

the lies I tell them are different
from the lies I tell myself
that by being both here and beyond
I am becoming a horizon

Yang San-Jih was not sure what these sentences meant, but reading the lines, he fell in love with the abstract scenes immediately. There were also analyses of novels and short stories of resistance. He wished he had a chance to read them all. Yang San-Jih read the anthology more than once, and marked it with a lot of notes. For the parts he did not understand, he would insert a piece of notepaper on the page as a mark so he would read them again. He kept the book as long as the library allowed and determined he should borrow it again after he read more about related topics.

If literature can be a tool of resistance against unfair situations, or a condemnation of injustice, then his published story might help expose corruption. To plot this story, Yang had interviewed his cousin many times. She helped him get a very clear picture of how businesses dealt with the extorting tax collectors. But in order to protect his cousin, he changed her company from a textile importer to an electronic factory. And in truth, his cousin did not quit. She was still working for the same company and buying off the tax collectors every two months.

Works of literature are often referenced to identify various aspects of a society, and fiction can help shed light on the basic understanding of a culture. Literature has always been a source of exploring the image of a country and its governing body. The image of a government presented in literature reflects the widely shared beliefs of the public, which also contributes to the stability of the society.

Chiang Sung-Nien wrote this opening paragraph of his report based on an essay "Literature, Culture, and the National Image" by an American author. He found it in an anthology he picked up randomly from the bookshelves in the library. Chiang Sung-Nien thought it was a good start, although he had no idea where it was leading to. He had gone to the library and found several books about literature, thinking they might be helpful for his report. He knew very little about literature, but since Yang San-Jih's work had been published by a major newspaper, it must be considered a recognized literary work. He actually enjoyed reading it, despite the fact that some episodes were too real to be comfortable for its readers.

> *Although "The Tax Collector" by Yang San-Jih is a work of fiction, it does have the potential to disquiet the harmony that our society has exerted such effort to create.*

Yes. Social harmony is the most important thing. Anyone endangering it should be checked, Chiang thought satisfactorily.

> *Fiction can instigate doubt, doubt as to the leadership of our government, doubt as to the patriotism of our nation. And undoubtedly, making up stories is inherently a political action.*

This paragraph was Chiang's alteration of the writing about fiction and politics by a Pakistani writer, which was part of the collection within the anthology. The author was actually taking an opposite perspective on fiction—he was crediting novelists who tried to change the world with fictional plots. To Chiang's astonishment, there were actually quite a few authors taking a similar stand in this anthology. This perspective seemed unheard of, or at least never talked about in the world that was familiar to Chiang: writing fiction could be activism. Another essay mentioned an American novel, *The Jungle,* which revealed the horrible conditions of a food factory in Chicago and became a bestseller, eventually fueling an investigation ordered by the White House. Subsequently, laws on the sanitation of food processing and improvement of working conditions were enacted.

It blew Chiang's mind. He had never been a literature lover and knew nothing about literary writers or their motivation in writing. He just thought novels or short stories were tales, and poems were about the beautiful things or sad feelings the poets echoed. He deliberated carefully about what to write in his report so he wouldn't get himself in trouble. Literature is powerful, was that why the Domestic Security Office got so nervous about Yang's story?

> *It is possible that fiction, even if it is not based on real incidents, can mislead the readers into thinking that the stories really did happen. Yang San-Jih's short story "The Tax Collector" libels governmental officials, erodes people's*

trust in the government, and breaks social harmony.

Writing this, Chiang wondered what would happen if a company reported the tax collectors' extortion to their supervisors? And just as he was assigned to spy on the employees of the Sino Petroleum, were those tax collectors also under watch? But it was not his business to tell the Domestic Security Office how to operate the government. He and his colleagues were asked to find problems, not to propose ideas regarding how to solve the problems. Chiang felt confused and absurd seeing his colleagues sitting in the bleak office, each of them working endlessly on reports for such obscure purposes. Nevertheless, in the conclusion of his report, Chiang Sung-Nien suggested that the Domestic Security Office should issue an executive order to the Independent Daily that, for the sake of maintaining the peace of the society, any of Yang San-Jih's writings should be reviewed by the Office before publishing.

Chiang returned the anthology as soon as he completed his report. His thoughts were disturbed by what he had read in the collection, and he wondered how a publication like this had been translated and published in Taiwan. "The examples in it were so inappropriate for Taiwan." He told himself. When he put it on the library cart for returned books, a small piece of notepaper fluttered out. He did not notice it as he quickly walked away from what troubled him.

Mr. President

Right after Duan Ming-Chuan was elected president of the National Taiwan Association of Journalism, news surfaced that he had taken money from the Hualien governors decades previously. A published graph showing how much money Duan had received annually was circulated online. It showed that over a fourteen year period, Duan had taken money equal to ten to twenty thousand US dollars each year, throughout the terms of four different Hualien governors.

Yi-Ting was in the US, covering news about the presidential election the day she read the online news about Duan. She was surprised. Yi-Ting had worked under Duan for 4 years for the East Coast Daily, her first job after leaving school. She had had an on-again-off-again affair with Duan for some of the time when he had allegedly taken the money. She had learned a lot from Duan about the reality of being a reporter, like the shrewdness required when handling facts versus opinions, and knowing what to present and what to withhold. Duan had insisted that in spite of what she had learned from her textbooks, integrity was not necessarily a cornerstone of her occupation. But at that time she had no idea that her supervisor and lover was being given handsome allowances that almost equaled her whole year's income. It wasn't actually a lot of money, but what was it for? And why was it never talked about until now, nearly twenty years later, as Duan was taking on the position of president of the association?

Driving across the US and observing numerous campaign events, Yi-Ting had a problem understanding why Donald Trump had made it all the way to the GOP nomination. She had believed there would be many Republicans opposing Trump and pulling him down at the last moment, but it never happened. Unlike many reports describing Trump supporters as low income, poorly educated blue collar workers, she had actually met a lot of well-educated, well-to-do people who gave her all kinds of reasons why they supported Trump. But none of them were convincing. Yi-Ting began to suspect that these people were actually too embarrassed to admit the real reasons they supported Trump, so they made up all kinds of empty excuses. Yi-Ting was more and more convinced that the Trump opposition was hitting at the wrong targets all the time. The debates, the fact-checking, the mocking, criticisms and condemnations were never the real concerns of Trump supporters.

So what were the actual reasons for their support of Trump? Human minds are sometimes too complicated to explore, especially on the dark side. For more than half a century, American society had operated according to political correctness. That sensibility at least muffled the sounds of hatred, discrimination, and open hostility even if it didn't help relieve the clashes caused by misunderstanding or ignorance. But now it was as if a giant crack in political correctness had unleashed an opportunity for people to finally vent their resentments brazenly. But there were so many people who were models of society, who appeared to be highly successful, as students, as parents, as employees, who never really made it clear why they would support a volatile, incoherent man to lead their country.

The next day in the online news, Yi-Ting read that the Hualien County Government issued a statement claiming that all the payments made to Duan Ming-Chuan were for his studies on Hualien's public policies. That was certainly news to Yi-Ting. For the 4 years they had worked together, she had never been aware of any studies that Duan had been conducting on Hualien's public policies. Duan was a man with great self-confidence, sometimes a little bit too flamboyant in her eyes. He was most proud of the fact that he had never had to work as hard as other reporters, "I don't have to dig up news; news come to me," he would say. If the statement by the Hualien County Government was true, that the payments were equal to a whole year's salary for a young reporter, Duan would have had to produce an academic thesis every year for 14 years in a row. And he would have still been working for the newspaper at the same time. How this was possible? And as a newspaper's staff reporter, was it ethical to be hired by another entity? Was his employer aware he was working for another organization?

Hualien County was blocked by the Central Range from the western part of Taiwan, thus it was less developed and the magnificent landscapes better conserved. Except, that is, for the notorious cement mines that decapitated the entire mountain. In every election, the right-wing conservatives always won the governor's race and took the majority of seats in the local council, because they repeatedly promised to improve the poor economy of Hualien. Yi-Ting suspected that the sense of poverty felt by Hualien's people was something they had been taught by these politicians. The public was told they were poor people and should feel ashamed of it, so their votes would go to the candidates who were claiming to save them from disgraceful poverty. But they were not truly poor. Decades had passed, and the economy was about the same, steady but not abundant. Huge developments hardly ever came to Hualien because it took too long for traffic to get there from the rest of the island. Local people were friendly to visitors from the cities because they were believed to be doing the local residents a favor just by coming there.

Yi-Ting applied for the job covering cultural news about Hualien because she thought it was a good place to live. It was quiet with almost no pollution, and rich with historical heritage that was still not fully understood, including the nearby traditional indigenous territories. Yi-Ting never figured out what brought Duan to Hualien. Both Duan and Yi-Ting were graduates from prestigious universities, and they earned their master degrees from the UK and the US respectively. Most of the journalists with comparable education would stay in Taipei, covering news of national significance. So, to be honest, they were treated like royalty in Hualien, a place believed to be inadequate for elites trying to establish a career.

Eight years ago, social media had brought significant change to the political landscape, which contributed to Barack Obama's victory. But was there any evident change now? Every day news poured out from all the news media, including mainstream, independent and social media, exposing Trump's sexist, racist, and xenophobic remarks, as well as the bankruptcy and tax evasion of his kingdom-like corporations. But it stood in contrast to Yi-Ting's personal experience of hearing people around her saying how Trump was going to reconstruct a stronger, better disciplined and more powerful United States.

"You don't mind his open discrimination against

immigrants?" She asked a Taiwanese man, Jack Shen, who had moved to the US eighteen years ago in order to provide a better education for his two children.

"He is rude, but he is an excellent negotiator; he manages things in a smart way."

How smart could a man be whose relentless rudeness often bordered on cruelty? "What is smart about the way he manages things?" Yi-Ting pursued,

But the man couldn't make himself clear. Jack lived in a gated community in Orange County, California. Yi-Ting noticed that the community consisted of mostly white people and Asian people. Asian Americans here sent their children to top public schools and top state universities, and hoped their opportunities wouldn't be shared with Hispanic Americans or African Americans. Typical middle-class, Yi-Ting thought to herself: hard-working, self-assured, responsible and law-abiding, but never feeling they possess enough to share with people less prestigious than they are.

"He pays a much lower tax rate than you do.

Doesn't that bother you?" Yi-Ting interviewed a young woman, Michelle, who was shopping in a Walmart in Phoenix, Arizona.

"As long as he's avoiding taxes legally, I don't mind."

"Can you avoid taxes legally too?" Yi-Ting asked.

"No. I don't know how to do that." Michelle shook her head.

There was no doubt that in Michelle's mind, a person who knew how to avoid paying taxes was more admirable than questionable. Yi-Ting felt frustrated. Did these people see that if wealthy people like Trump paid higher tax rates, just a little bit higher, it would be a large amount of money compared to their incomes? Michelle was paying almost two and a half months of her salary. With that amount of money she could have a comfortable vacation in Europe, or alternatively, she could work only nine and a half months a year if she knew how to avoid paying the tax.

The news continued to confuse Yin-Ting.

Everyday anyone could find hundreds of examples of evidence that Trump was a sexist, a racist, and a tax evader, and it never changed the determination of his voters.

"Do you agree with the idea of building a wall between the border of the USA and Mexico?" Yi-Ting interviewed Samuel, a car mechanic in Las Vegas, a man in his fifties who was earning almost three times the minimum hourly wage because of his experience and excellent skills.

"Yes, I do"

"Why?"

"The undocumented immigrants steal our jobs."

"How so? There is no wall between Canada and America, Canadians don't steal jobs?"

Samuel wasn't sure. He searched to come up with another idea. "The wall is for the security of our homeland."

"How is that?" Yi-Ting felt this nice guy seemed like he was facing a test. His mind was rummaging through possible answers for the questions the teacher was throwing at him. She took out her tablet and presented Samuel the charts she had found, "This study shows that the crimes committed by undocumented immigrants are significantly lower than native-born Americans."

Samuel was not interested. Yi-Ting was more and more convinced that people had decided to support Trump before they had even started trying to formulate any of their reasons. And she still had no idea what the real reasons were for their support.

Meanwhile, there was not much progress in Duan Ming-Cuan's news. Duan's opposers demanded that the Hualien County Government should present the study reports that Duan had provided. They wanted to see what kinds of reports were worth so much money. But the County Government said they had mixed Duan's papers with other texts, so it was impossible to distinguish Duan's contribution from others.

When Yi-Ting was working under Duan, Duan always told her that reporters should learn how to raise issues. At first Yi-Ting did not understand that Duan's idea of "raising" issues did not mean to bring up issues, but to "foster" issues. He meant to hold back information until small incidents became major crises so they could have inside stories for exclusive reports. Was that what he meant when he said he never had to pursue the news, because the news pursued him?

They did have very different perspective about their work. In the case of insignificant stories that Yi-Ting considered unworthy of attention, Duan might cover them for several days. But then when she believed something should undergo in-depth investigation, Duan handled it like a trivial matter. One example was when the scandal exploded about the Governor's right hand man taking bribes. Duan never pursued it; he simply rewrote it based on the reports of other news media. And the totally corrupt construction of low-income housing was nothing but an insignificant mistake under Duan's pen.

Several years later Yi-Ting realized that to her, Duan was an OK lover, but not an OK supervisor or colleague. Had they engaged in different professions, their relationship might have been smoother. Duan read a lot of history; he particularly liked the power struggles in ancient Chinese courts. Yi-Ting remembered that books about power wrestling, wars, coups, or revolutions were everywhere in his place. He read them many times and remembered them well. He liked to give historical examples during their conversations, but Yi-Ting usually failed to catch his points. Yi-Ting did not recall seeing any publications of contemporary issues in Duan's place. He never read anything about economics, sociology or political science. Traces of his involvement with other women, like a mascara tube found under the bed, or an earring forgotten in the bathroom, were more obvious than any evidence that Duan had ever studied Hualien's public policies. Regardless, Duan was a fun man to be around in general, no matter whether Yi-Ting was jealous or excited or frustrated. But the gap between their perceptions of their careers obstructed them from building a more trusting intimacy. After working together and sometimes sleeping together for 4 years, Yi-Ting finally left the job and cut off their affair. Or did the end of their affair end her job? She was never sure.

Yi-Ting's executive editor in Taiwan complained

that she only covered Trump's supporters. "Are you becoming his fan, too?"

Yi-Ting laughed out loud. She understood Hillary Clinton's supporters, but she did not understand Trump's supporters. She had great interest in these people, but at the same time she detested their tolerance of Trump's sexism and racism. Yi-Ting thought to herself that if her editor wanted stories about Clinton's supporters, she could write about them without even interviewing them.

Suddenly it dawned on Yi-Ting that perhaps that was how Duan practiced his profession. The point was not what he reported, but what he did not report. If Trump's supporters did not mind his hateful remarks, then updating similar remarks daily, even hourly, wouldn't change their minds. Nevertheless the tweets and remarks were good material for the news media. Opponents would read them, curse them, and post them on social media. Then there were more readers and more shares. A lazy reporter could just follow hateful remarks to attract more readers. After all, the advertisers of news media hired the websites with the greatest numbers of clicks, not the most professional journalism. In the same way that twenty years ago Duan was paid off to play down certain topics in his reports, reporters today were not pursuing critical issues of public interest, but simply the readers' attention. The more controversial, the better.

Bad dramas always attracted a greater audience. Yi-Ting felt defeated.

Duan never made any statement regarding doubt about his past conduct. And opinions supporting Duan began to emerge. A group of reporters said Duan's payments were earned by his talents, and no matter what he had written for the Hualien County Government, he certainly was not overpaid. They added that those who criticized him were simply jealous. Did Duan motivate these younger reporters to express their support? Nay. Yi-Ting did not think so. Duan was too proud to ask for favors like this.

A middle-aged local Hualien reporter, Chan Ta-Chung, said he remembered helping to compile Duan's reports, and they were informational, insightful, and very valuable. What the fuck? So those who have captured dubious gains are worshipped, not questioned. Yi-Ting thought of Michelle. What an odd mentality demonstrated by otherwise ordinary, well-intentioned people. None of the members of this group supporting Duan faced the fact that it was not about whether Duan was overpaid or not.

Yi-Ting remembered Chan, a small man with indigenous parentage. He knew many things: plants, animals, local histories and local people. Yi-Ting had learned a lot from him. Chan liked to hang out with Duan and Yi-Ting, but Duan never seemed to care about Chan's contribution even though Chan had provided him quite useful information about local events, such as who had rough patches, with whom, and for what. Yi-Ting still remembered the contemptuous look Duan had one time when Chan brought him a bottle of wine. She knew Chan was hurt, and she was hurt, too. Yi-Ting drank it with Chan. It was not a heavenly drink, but she had never needed high-end wines to celebrate friendship.

By now Yi-Ting was quite sure that the so-called studies and papers supposedly composed by Duan for the Haulien County Government never ever existed. So what was Chan doing now? Chan still cared about

Duan's opinions of him. When Yi-Ting realized that Chan had lied for Duan about the reports, she concluded that Chan had never given up his quest to earn more recognition from him. But it was not going to work. Yi-Ting knew that the more humble a person was with Duan, the less respect he could win from him. She felt so sorry for Chan. With the knowledge he had accumulated from his hard work and inherited from his folks, he could have made himself a much more worthy journalist.

In November, as Yi-Ting predicted, Trump won. And Duan was inaugurated as the president of the National Taiwan Association of Journalism. The questionable events of twenty years ago were never explained by Duan, but by that time few still cared.

The Surveillance

Report by J(code)
Event: Reading Club
Date and Time: 9:30~11:30p.m. Nov 28, 1979
Venue: Aunty Meifang's Eatery after dinner service
Watching Target: H(code)
Number of Participants: Around 20 people

Kao Heh-Shun(host of the reading) explained that the Taiwanese government recently has strengthened its ties with the South African government because these two entities are sort of isolated from international society. The former was because its seat in the United Nations has been replaced by China, the later because of the segregation between white and colored peoples. Thus there are exchanges for a variety of businesses between the two countries, including the publishing industry. Unfortunately, as both societies are under censorship, many publications on sensitive issues are not allowed to be published. Kao has some books brought to him from London by his foreign friends, and he will introduce them in the future gatherings of this reading club. The first book Kao introduced was about a family of British descendants who fought for the rights of colored people.

H left before the end of the reading, the reason was not clear.

Conclusion: The goals of this reading club and Kao's purposes need further observation.

This report is presented to the Squad No. 13, Taiwan Police Command.

Report by C(code)
Event: Reading Club
Date and Time: 9:30~11:30p.m. Nov 28, 1979
Venue: Aunty Meifang's Eatery
Watching Target: J(code)
Number of Participants: 23 men and women

Kao Heh-Shun introduced the novel *Burger's Daughter* by South African writer Nadine Gordimer and read several pieces he had translated into

Taiwanese. This book was about the anti-apartheid movement by Afirkaaners. Rosa, Burger's daughter, recalled her father who had been sentenced to lifetime and later died in prison.

Kao Heh-Shun pointed out that, although the authorities were disturbed by Burger's anti-apartheid efforts, he was charged as a communist party member. Therefore in the court he couldn't openly debate the reasons why he was against apartheid and risked his wellbeing for other peoples.

This book was published in London earlier this year, Kao said, and it is banned in South Africa.

J raised several questions about the formation of the fiction. He also asked Kao whether if the book was translated into Chinese and published in Taiwan, would it be banned as well. Kao said it would very likely be banned because Taiwan's government was friendly to the South African government while other countries condemned its apartheid.

Conclusion: ~~Although law and order are important, humanity to all is fundamental.~~ Although humanity to all is important, law and order are fundamental.

This report is presented to the Security Office, Taiwan Investigation Bureau.

Report by D(code)
Event: Reading Club
Date and Time: 9:30~11:30p.m. Nov 28, 1979
Venue: An eatery after dinner service
Watching Target: C(code)
Number of Participants: Around 30

Kao Heh-Shun read several paragraphs from a book "The Daughter of Burger" by a woman writer from South Africa. Burger and his wife were communists, they'd done things to subvert the government but were arrested and put in jail. After both of them died, their daughter Rosa ran to Europe and met a man. They had a romantic affair before she returned to South Africa, where her life was constricted by close surveillance.

C did not interact with the speaker or others, but he took notes from time to time.

Conclusion: The intention of Kao's demonstration of this book is unclear, but C seemed to be intrigued by it and divulged sympathy to the characters.

This report is presented to the Squad No. 05, Taiwan Police Command.

Report by S(code)
Event: Reading Club
Date and Time: 9:30~11:30p.m. Nov 28, 1979
Venue: Aunty Meifang's Eatery after dinner service
Watching Target: D(code)
Number of Participants: 18 men & 7 women

A realistic South African novel about Rosa Burger's family conducting underground activities to shake the segregation of people of different ethnicities was read by Kao Heh-Shun(host): After her parents were persecuted and passed away, Rosa went to UK, but her open activities were criticized as honoring herself for being the daughter of martyrs by her childhood friend, a black man, whose relatives were all killed by their anti-apartheid actions back in South Africa. Therefore Rosa decided not to meet up with her lover in Paris, instead she returned to South

Africa, knowing she would be under the surveillance of the authorities again.

D attended this reading with several acquaintances whose identities are unknown. He dozed off in the second hour.

Conclusion: D seemed to be in such a reading before. What they had read previously needs to be found out.

This report is presented to the Security Office, Taiwan Investigation Bureau.

Report by H(code)
Event: Reading Club
Date and Time: 9:30~11:30p.m. Nov 28, 1979
Venue: Aunty Meifang's Eatery
Watching Target: S(code)
Number of Participants: 28 people, 4 of them took off earlier

A fiction *Burger's Daughter* by Ms. Gordimer was read by the host of the reading Kao Heh-Shun, who translated it from South African English into

Taiwanese. This book is recommended by Kao, for it looks into several delicate political issues in South Africa. In the future readings he will recommend more South African literature, especially those about the inequality between different ethnicities.

After the reading, questions regarding colonialism were brought up. Colonialism in Taiwan was not a strange topic, but there are some issues Kao said he'd rather talk about in private.

Conclusion: It is obvious that Kao Heh-Shun is recruiting members for certain political groups and he uses book reading clubs to attract people who might join him. S did not show enthusiasm during the reading.

This report is presented to the Squad No. 9, Taiwan Police Command.

While translating and flipping over the book, Kao Heh-Shun recollected the question he was asked during the reading. How on earth fiction is formulated?

Marketing

Opinions for the Committee of Publication Examination

Date: 1978/Nov/11

Reviewer Code: M1010

This is a historical novel with a background of the French Revolution and how people from the bottom rungs of society rose up to overturn the monarchy. However, in a time when the threat of the communist regimes is so tense as it is today, our priority must be to enforce the social order. Thus I cannot suggest publishing such a book that in no way helps our crucial mission of stomping out the persistent and existential threat of global communism.

Date: 1978/Nov/12

Reviewer Code: M1021

This fiction is about low lifes, hobos, whores, and shoplifters, not to mention the fact that is filled with a string of vulgar vocabulary. I don't see any merit in this work. It will rot the mentality of the already decadent public, and wear down their will to have a more uplifting life and contribute more to their country.

Date: 1978/Nov/14
Reviewer Code: M2221

This is an outstanding work with very high artistic merit. All the leading characters and their situations draw references to identifiable characters in our contemporary society. Through these extremely marginalized people, the author cleverly leads the readers to see the dilemma and wisdom of life and the inequality between social classes. I give it five stars and hope to see its success in the publishing market.

***

The secretary finished typing the report from the previous week and stamped the conclusion marking the fate of this novel: BANNED. Even without the real identities of these reviewers, she knew very well who they were. The code M1010 was that of a literature professor who showed little passion in literature. His opinions were usually worthless. The code M1021 referred to a reporter from the newspaper founded by the ruling party who knew more about propaganda than journalism. And the code M2221 indicated a self-made essayist and a real literature critic but one whose contributions were hardly recognized. He was included as a reviewer for the fake diversity of the Committee.

She collected her stuff and called it a day from work. When she walked through the night market near her home to find some food for dinner, she checked at the back of a general stall of cheap products, where piles of used or unsold books like comics, fashion magazines and romantic stories were for sale. Beside the wall, a pile of unauthorized copies of the book she just reported on were advertised as: "Newly Banned!" And the price was doubled from the previous week.

Life Looked at Through A Single Window

The draft of the book *Youth Taiwan* has laid on my desk for more than a week now. I shouldn't have promised the publishing house to write the introduction for it, I have no idea how to start. *Youth Taiwan* contains the stories of three young singers in the 60s in Taiwan, they performed in cheap underground shows, singing banned Japanese songs for the elderly who grew up during the Japanese colonial rule. A romantic plot, but it could be read critically.

This is a reprint, the original book was published in the 70s. The author Jaddy Fu had very few literary works but in recent years they unexpectedly became a hot target of academic research. Many said his writings had been underrated, quite a few scholars analyzed his style as modernism that blended realistic incidents with fictional scenes, or vice versa. They praised him as a pioneer of Taiwanese-style modernist literature, but one who was unfortunately overlooked because of the isolation of Taiwan's literary society during his time. Over the past two decades, as more and more writers throughout the world were introduced to Taiwan, Jaddy Fu's books had become surprisingly acclaimed among young readers who could access world literature easily. Publishers competed for the copyright to reprint Jaddy Fu's works, some of them had become best sellers for weeks.

My memory of Jaddy Fu who died in 1998 was not his literary achievement, but the brief speech he had made in the ceremony of the Golden Leaf Film Awards in 1982, of which I was one of the judges. He was given the award for Best Screenplay. I remember when his name was announced, he walked to the stage, smoothed his jacket placidly before taking over the golden leaf trophy from the presenter and the microphone from the hostess, and said, "I've written a nearly perfect screenplay, but to be perfect, any limitation on speech and creativity should be removed." He held the trophy to the air and lifted up his voice, "Say NO to censorship!" The ceremony froze for several seconds, until the hostess got her composure back and said in an obviously fake cheerful voice,

"Congratulations. And let's go to the next program." The audience applauded when the lighting on the stage blinked twice to suggest the coming show, a folk dance celebrating harvest. Girls hardly having any experience of farming jumped in to the stage with bright clothes and bamboo hats. They wore exaggerated smiles on their faces.

The next day the three major newspapers reported the news of the awards with much less coverage compared to the previous years. Of course Jaddy Fu's demand for the termination of censorship was not mentioned at all. A picture of the winning drama movie A Battle for the Republic of China was the only image published about the ceremony. In the late afternoon, the Independent Evening News had a small block on Jaddy Fu's speech and a brief introduction of his award winning screenplay. There was not a picture of Jaddy Fu or the film based on his work.

The speech Jaddy Fu made did not change anything about the control over speeches and publications in Taiwan, instead, it ended his writing career. The publishing industry stopped contacting him, and of course no film producer would engage him again.

But, honestly, what had happened to Jaddy Fu was never my concern. At that time I wasn't even aware of how it impacted him. Almost 40 years later, Jaddy Fu's posthumous success reminds me of what had happened to me and I feel a little bit ashamed. I am ashamed of myself that I only thought about myself at that time, like, when someone gives your boat a push to the ocean and you're totally unaware of the effort, ignoring the expansiveness of the unusual scenes.

I was in my early thirties, and had just finished my doctoral degree in literature and started teaching in two colleges as a part-time lecturer. I published several papers, gave speeches about movies based on novels to student clubs or reading groups of engineers. I dressed like a British literary professor—tweed blazer with elbow patches that usually was too hot to wear in this subtropical island. In today's terms, I would certainly be called a hipster. I did not want to be seen as belonging to my peers, a group of hardworking researchers without imagination, without ambition, and without personal taste.

I was the only one without a film background on the jury of the 1982 Golden Leaf Film Awards because the award organizers thought they needed to have a more diverse jury board and a scholar of literature could tell them more about screenplays. I sat with the other 14 judges for three days, watching all the 35 nominated films. I had no idea about film making, but contributed as much as I could by providing some opinions about the narrative structures, such as how the scenarios unfolded along or against time axises. I did not know how much of my opinions had influenced the final decisions, but was thrilled to be with famous directors, critics, actors and actresses who were also judges because they had won the awards in previous years. I couldn't help but comparing the images of them I saw from mass media and in person. But at that time I never admitted that I was excited. I told myself that I was the only judge from the academic world and my value in being with the rest of them was my identity as an outsider. So a lot of time I just paid no heed to who they were... uh, I should say I tried hard to pay no heed to who they were. A lot of times I pretended I even did not know who they were. I imagined that they would know me after the ceremony, after all I provided my academic perspective.

The annual Golden Leaf Film Festival probably

was the largest event of the entire cultural industry in Taiwan at that time, given that no new TV channel or newspaper could be established due to martial law. At that time the largest film producer in Taiwan was a state-own company, few other businesses had capital enough to make movies. Each year before the ceremony, the three TV channels and four newspapers would report on the festival daily, accompanied with an introduction of blockbuster American films of the year. In 1982 the most popular movies were E.T., Star Trek, and An Officer and A Gentleman. But I focused on Sophie's Choice, which was adapted from William Styron's novel.

Looking back, if I don't be honest with myself I would fall into the same feeling of shame again. My service in the board of judges did bring me illusions that I might step into a new phase of my career, making me different from my fellow scholars who knew nothing but their own professions, who knew nobody but their own kind.

Vanity, yes. And vanity is very much about illusion. How come I believed an event like this could bring me to another place, another status? But at that time I did eagerly expect to turn a new page of my life. I told myself perhaps I did not have to find a full-time professorship in a college, I might become a columnist, an author of fiction and cinema, a critic, and a popular speaker. I should write more about Sophie's Choice, I told myself, and I should also look into earlier movies, such as The French Lieutenant's Woman. I really liked Maryl Streep, although I found the movies totally deviated from the novels.

But I never became a movie critic, or a columnist, or a popular speaker. It took me another two years to get a full-time teaching position in a polytech, and another five years to transfer to a university. I earned my professorship by publishing papers on Taiwanese literature in the 1930s, nothing to do with cinema at all. I am the author of two books of early modern Taiwanese literature, the kind of publications that no one would read except a few graduate students. I hardly made speeches outside of my classrooms and hung out with researchers who were as boring as I was. I advised students who needed to get degrees as soon as possible, and helped them to see the reality of academic society. I have an average marriage, I raised two normal children, provided them standard education. Now I am even a grandfather of three kids who I still have problem remembering what grades they are at in school. Before I retired, I completed task after task and dragged on my long teaching occupation day by day without dreaming to have a life different to what I was having. I was content with what I had, although from time to time I had to appear like I was going to accomplish more if the conditions for research were better, if there were more grants for my projects, or if students worked harder, or the administration of the university was less bureaucratic. But if one really wants to criticise me, he or she certainly would say I never ever stepped out of my comfort zone. You know the largest comfort zone is called "mainstream", right?

And this is not what I feel ashamed of, no one should be ashamed of his or her unambitious career or unimaginative life. What I am feeling ashamed of is a combination of many things, but mostly how I first felt about Jaddy Fu's shouting words in the Golden Leaf Awards ceremony 37 years ago. For a period of time, two years I think, because I couldn't land a full-time job for two years, I believed that my plan to be a movie expert was grounded because of Jaddy Fu.

Because of his unaligned performance during the ceremony, the government shrunk its support of the event in the following years in order to penalize the event organizers' failure to control the situation. The cinema industry had been quiet for several years, big investment like The Battle for the Republic of China hadn't happened again. Less grants were awarded for filmmaking, fewer foreign movies were imported, especially those touching on political issues. Cinemas suffered from low incomes, many of them eventually were out of business. All these gave me reasons to suspect that my difficulties in establishing a career in the cinema industry were the consequence of Jaddy Fu's rebellious speech. It made my inclusion of my contribution as a judge of the 1982 Golden Leaf Film Festival in my CV insignificant. It made my connection with people with big names in the cinema industry useless. My secretive celebration was aborted, my stories about those celebrities I encountered and worked together with never got chance to be told. My hope to be engaged as the consultant of film producers was never substantiated.

But I was only thirty-two or thirty-three years old when that happened. Any illusion or naivety or stupidity would be normal for any person in that age. My real regret is, it took me decades to understand that my obstacle toward a more celebrational lifestyle was not Jaddy Fu, but my own rejection of a broader view of reality, even years after my burst daydream. Five years after the film festival I participated in, martial law was abolished, thanks to the risky protest made one-after-another by people I did not know, and in another five years the censorship of all cultural products was lifted. I called myself lucky that my own research never triggered the alarm of governmental control, but was that purely luck? A cow can stay one hundred percent safe from an electric fence without even acknowledging it exists.

What would happen if Jaddy Fu never had the speech? Would I become a film expert and have a lot of job engagements? The government wouldn't decrease its investment in this industry, and I might be commissioned to take on some exciting projects. But this assumption is valueless today. In the early 80s even if the resources from the public sector to the film industry had not been withdrawn, it would have been for nothing but stronger propaganda. Even if my career dream was not damaged by Jaddy Fu's unwelcomed talk, I might have found myself unfit to Taiwan's market after all.

The real question that I really should have asked but never asked until recently was, what would happen if the rest of the audience in the 1982 ceremony did not respond to Jaddy Fu's talk with silence? When everyone maintained silence for fearing the situation might turn ugly, the boat sank slowly.

I sit down on my desk and type, "Jaddy Fu's *Youth Taiwan* implicated the infantile society of Taiwan." Even today, few see the paradox that resistance against Japanese colonial rule was encouraged, resistance against the repression over free speech of the Republic of China was a taboo.

I know the editor asked me to write something about this book not because she knew I had contributed Jaddy Fu's winning of the Golden Leaf, it was simply because I have more time to write in my retired life. She probably had inquired to other scholars with no avail. Can I write something smart, smart enough to be my small, secretive redemption?

I decide to get some fresh air first, perhaps I should take a walk to the grocery at the street corner to buy myself some beer for my writing. I grab a jacket from my wardrobe, a corduroy blazer with elbow patches, to put on. It is so worn out now, it perfectly suits a retired literature professor well, totally out of fashion, and totally oblivious to his unknown guilt.

The Hunger Devil

Ah-Zhan woke up from the smell of milkfish porridge, the tenderness of the fish belly in the long-cooked rice was hot enough to burn the tongue, and the green onions had greatly enriched the flavors. As she opened her eyes, sunlight had begun to climb over the high windows. She sat up and looked around, all the others were still asleep. She jumped down from the bunk bed as quietly as possible and walked toward the restroom shared by more than thirty women.

The breakfast was very dry buns, shredded pork with cucumber preserved in soy sauce, and peanuts that tasted mildewy. The pork and preserved cucumber were too salty, Ah-Zhan had to drink a lot of cold water to wash it down. But at least she had regular meals. The memory of hunger was not a fond one at all.

When Ah-Zhan was in high school, she had grown tall enough to help her father and other milkfish farmers work in the pond they created together. It was the time when the farmlands along the west coast had sunken to lower than the sea level, and the soil turned too saline to grow anything. Later their fish farm was accused of being the cause of the land sinking because they pumped underground water to fill the pond. But they had to give up rice farming in the first place because their lands sank, so who should be responsible for it?

Ah-Zhan's father and other farmers spent a lot of time and money to learn how to convert their rice fields into a fish pond for all the families to rely on the income they might make by the quantities of fish they could raise. For the first several years, they made a lot of mistakes, like the time the water leaked through the clay walls they erected by hand, or when the feed they produced was not right for the fish and the water was polluted, or the season they waited for too long to harvest the fish which were still too small resulting in them finally dying in the winter chill.

Later they were taught to put a thin layer of water into the pond first during the end of winter to cultivate algae. When spring started, the water would be dried by sunlight and wind, and at that time they spread rice bran for the growth of more algae. They then added a thin layer of water again, while waiting until the pond dried up once more, so that it should not dry too fast or too slowly. If it dried too fast, they'd add more water, if it dried too slowly, they'd drain the pond. They were told if the soil at the bottom of the pond was barren, they should spread more rice bran, but since they did not have so much rice bran, they added chicken manure. They also found, after trial and error, that the chicken manure must be fermented prior to use, otherwise the fish might die because of the lack of oxygen. They had to watch the quality of the pond water closely, if there was too much algae, fish would tend to gather on the water surface and become the prey of egrets or seagulls.

Diseases were another challenge, the fast reproduction of euglena or dinoflagellates might cause the death of a great amount of fish, in this case the only solution was to use chemicals to kill them.

How is the fish farming at home now? How are those hard-working fish farmers? Ah-Zhan thought. Do they know where I am? Are they in trouble because of me?

Ah-Zhan had been imprisoned for nine months, and she has no idea how much longer she would be there. Her lawyer Gee Sheen, a volunteer, had visited her four times, but had very little information he could give her. They did not know when a trial would proceed, if there was going to be a trial at all. Most of the evidence in favor of her or her peers had been eradicated by the staff from the so called National Security Agency during her time on the run. Mr. Gee Sheen's visits were rather to give her support than legal service, and to show to the authorities that Ah-Zhan was not by herself, and they should not bully her.

Finishing her dried bun, the peanuts and the very salty preserved dish, Ah-Zhan still felt hungry. She might have stared at the other inmate's food too obviously without her own awareness, Hsiao Jin, a middle-aged woman, pushed her breakfast to Ah-Zhan, "I don't need so much food, take it for me. You are young, you need more energy." Ah-Zhan felt embarrassed, but she devoured down Hsiao Jin's food immediately. Her mind must have been more hungry than her body.

During the weeks of Ah-Zhan's running and hiding in the forest, finding food was the most difficult thing. At first she received meat jerky, rice balls or bananas from time to time that were hung over a tree not far from the road, supplied by people unknown to her. Later the food stopped coming, and she waited but nothing more came, Ah-Zhan decided it meant she needed to run again, assuming it meant either her food supplier was in trouble, or she was warned not to stay in the same place.

She climbed up to the higher mountain, assuming that the deeper inside the forest she retreated, the safer she would be. She found a flat place not too far from a stream where she could crash under two leaning rocks, a spot away from the gusty wind. But what to eat became a problem. Ah-Zhan did not possess much knowledge about the wilderness and had prepared for nothing for her run into the mountains. When their procession in the name of anti-corruption and transparent policy-making was broken down by armed law enforcement, several demonstrators were picked up by police with great force. Ah-Zhan was stunned, she never really expected such a conflict could happen, after all, they only demanded a government with integrity. Which society doesn't need an honest government? When Ah-Zhan was trying to assist a man who was pulled and lifted by a bunch of policemen, Da Chuan grabbed her arm and pushed her away, "Run! Wait for messages in the Monkey Mountain." He pointed at a direction, where another man led her away from the scene of the beating and screaming.

Ah-Zhan entered the mountain like a running mouse, she was by herself, those who had travelled together earlier disappeared without her notice. What was the next step? She walked along the mountain trails all night but stayed close to the areas where she still could see landmarks like a pavilion constructed by a nearby temple, or a lamppost suggesting a road under it. That was where she found the food delivered from time to time.

But contrary to her hopes of being able to get out and go home soon, the disruption to her food supply told her to run further from the town or any settlement. In the depth of a forest, everything was so different to things she was used to seeing and feeling in the city. Light from the moon and stars was faint, there were sounds of birds and bugs, activities of unknown animals… in the night Ah-Zhan was easily scared by any movement of the things surrounding her like the scraping branches of trees swaying in the breeze.

There are so many messages in the gusts of wind at night, too bad that Ah-Zhan couldn't decipher them. What happened? Should she get down to check it out? Could she go back to the place where she had found food to see if the supply had resumed? Or, was it possible for her to ask for something to eat from the nearest temple? She must look terrible now, people seeing her might report her as a loiterer, a trouble maker. Observing the activities of birds and squirrels, Ah-Zhan found some berries from the trees, but they hardly fed her. To save energy, she slept as much as she could. She kept telling herself not to think about food, to persuade herself, her mind and her body, that she could sustain her life without food.

Ah-Zhan lost track of the date. She must have been on the run for weeks. How would she know when she could go back? Who would know where she was? It was getting colder—was it September or October? What would happen if she still couldn't go home in winter?

One night Ah-Zhan's lower belly cramped, she could hardly stand or sit straight. Then a flow of warm liquid was felt between her legs. Her period started. Ah-Zhan began to cry, she hadn't eaten normally for so long, and now she was losing the precious fluid from her body. Ah-Zhan found the only fabric she had with her to use as a sanitary pad, the cloth used for the last food delivery many days ago that was never taken back by her food supplier. The cramps were so bad, she usually took pain killers during the first two days of her period, now she had nothing to stop the sharp pain. Ah-Zhan's aunt Hsiu-Chun blamed her menstrual discomfort on her work in the water of their fishing pond, she said the coldness of water had penetrated her body, her womb, that not only caused her pain every month, but also would make her childbearing very difficult in the future. Aunt Hsiu-Chun told her parents more than once not to have Ah-Zhan work in the cold water, but who else could do it? They all had to climb up and down the pond, they couldn't afford to hire people.

Childbearing, Ah-Zhan laughed bitterly. Did her parents know where she was now? Did her fellow protestors know she was still on the run? Perhaps she should walk out no matter what would happen to her.

In prison at least Ah-Zhan was provided three meals a day, although the food was terrible. Mr. Gee Sheen once analyzed her situation and strategy of her trial, which eventually was to be scheduled due to the pressure brought by international human rights watchers. But it was a dilemma for Ah-Zhan. Mr. Gee Sheen told her that if she wanted to best defend herself and herself only, she could cooperate with the prosecutors. She could tell them what her organization meant to achieve, what orders she had been given, and who else she had worked with.

"What did we mean to achieve? Wasn't it clear that we want to have a corrupt-free government, we want to have transparent policy-making? We want democracy! We put all these on the handouts, on the banners, we talk about it all the time, it is not a secret!"

"I know. But they try to make it a conspiracy.

Sabotage of the government, and collusion of foreign power."

"It's not a conspiracy, nor sabotage. And it is just us, no foreign power!"

"You know what the prosecutors are heading for, they want to divide all the defendants and break down their solidarity."

"It is not working on me!" Ah-Zhan said with great fury.

"But if any of your accompanies cooperates, all of you lose your chance to get lenient sentences."

"One of us might betray the others?"

"Yes. And it is very likely."

"And if all of us are betrayers?"

"All of you will get serious punishment."

"I see. Some of us pay the price of being betrayed. And if all of us are betraying one another, we pay the price of being betrayed together."

After all, what they had demanded for would not be addressed by the government. To the government, corruption was not a problem, the problem was those people who tried to reveal it and correct it. And the mutual-trust of the protestors was tested, with the ugliest trick.

That night Ah-Zhan asked those sharing the same room with her if anyone knew how to cook milkfish porridge. One of the women inquired, "Why bother to know? You can't cook it here."

"I am afraid I will be imprisoned for the rest of my life."

All the women became quiet. In this place, inmates never discussed the reasons of their imprisonment, but from the casual chats, Ah-Zhan knew the crimes they had committed were mostly fraud, theft, abortion or prostitution. None of them had been, like her, put in jail because of a public demand for democracy and government reform. Would they understand?

Then one of the women, a mother in her forties, began to recite the recipe:

Scale the fish, wash it, cut it into halves, and remove the bones as cleanly as possible.

Wash it again and fillet the fish. Cook the fish in clear water with a medium fire for fifteen minutes.

Soak the rice in water for half an hour before boiling it with a medium flame.

Turn the flame down when the rice becomes gruel, add it to the milkfish soup.

Add thinly sliced fresh ginger, salt, white pepper powder, and rice wine.

Cook the porridge with low heat until the rice absorbs the flavor of the fish and ginger.

Add green onions just before serving it.

Ah-Zhan sighed, like she had just tasted the freshly cooked milkfish porridge and was satisfied. And every woman around her seemed to be relieved.

A Little Traitor

Chun-Hui was so shocked when she looked at the profile on the handouts the Director of Discipline brought on to the stage to show all of the students. It was an unkempt man with stubble that had begun to show on his cheeks. The Director announced: "If you see this man, you must report him to the police, or to your teachers." It was a black-and-white image caught by cctv, very blurred, but Chun-Hui had no problem recognizing it was Uncle Huang.

"These people are traitors, they are on the run. If they are not caught and put in jail, they will continue doing harmful things to our country." The Director of Discipline preached in a threatening tone as though among these elementary students there were accomplices of these traitors.

Before noon, a big sign was erected in front of the passageway between the classrooms and the garden, it read: "Concealing Espionage is Equal to Treason". The blood-red characters were terrifying, like they could become monsters any time to grab kids walking past it. The whole day Chun-Hui was ill at ease, she couldn't concentrate on the classes, and during the recesses, the fear of being grabbed by the red monsters waiting for her outside of the classrooms prevented her from doing anything. She did not understand the meaning of espionage or treason, but these two words were seen everywhere these days, from TV, newspapers, and banners over the gates of some buildings. But not until now did Chun-Hui realize it was about Uncle Huang.

She even did not dare to go to the restroom, the whole day she sat on her desk with her bladder getting fuller and fuller, and her mind less and less focusing on teachers' talks. The day of school seemed to be unusually long, Chun-Hui was on the edge of collapsing.

Chun-Hui had seen Uncle Huang almost every month, when he came to drink with her father. And they smoked. Dad usually did not smoke, but when Uncle Huang was around, they'd chain smoke all night. Chun-Hui did not like her dad smoking, so she did not like Uncle Huang. She suspected her mom also did not like Uncle Huang, because she complained about his visits more than once.

After school and at home, Mom was busy preparing dinner right after she returned from work. She was a clerk of the township office. Chun-Hui was going to ask Mom about Uncle Huang, but Mom bade her and her brother to start dinner without Dad.

"Where is dad?"

Mom thought for a moment and said, "An elderly relative in Kaohsiung was very ill, he went to assist him."

"When he will come back?"

Mom waited for a moment again, and said, "I don't know. Depends on how well or how bad the old man's health is."

Mom seemed to be in a low mood, Chun-Hui thought she'd better stay quiet. After dinner, she stayed in her small room all night. They lived in a packed apartment that her father and his brother inherited from their parents, and each month they paid some money to his father's brother for renting his share of the apartment. The furniture from the time of Chun-Hui's grandparents and their own mismatched, making their activities at home awkward, but they couldn't afford not to use the old furniture. The old furniture had better quality, but they were not designed for the space or for their needs. Several things in it were broken, like in the rainy season, water would drip from the northeast corner of the ceiling. But they never had it fixed, because her dad never got agreement on how he and his brother should split the expense. They let the rain drip for years, until the site next to their apartment was developed, a higher building was constructed and blocked their apartment from heavy rain, as well as sunlight. They did not paint the rain stains over. Chun-Hui gathered that their parents had a philosophy that if a problem was not fixed, it shouldn't be covered up even the symptoms stopped showing.

Chun-Hui took out her homework. In school her performance was just passable. As long as she was not punished for neglecting her assignments, she'd never bother to work harder in case teachers would notice her. Unlike most of the girls in her class who strove to impress their teachers, Chun-Hui maintained a distance from teachers and the Director of Discipline, Director of Curriculum, Director of This and Director of That. She participated in as few school activities as possible.

When Chun-Hui woke up from a horrifying dream, she realized she had fallen asleep when doing her homework. It was not done, but she was too tired to continue, she could hardly open her eyes. She had been running and running in her dream, and she wasn't clear what she was running away from. The blood-red monsters? The ghost taking shape from Uncle Huang's cigarette smoke? The Director of Discipline who found Chun-Hui had known Uncle Huang?

The next morning on her way to school, the same handout the Director of Discipline had shown them before became larger posters attached on to the public bulletin board of their community. Chun-Hui shuddered. Did her mother see it?

The big sign of "Concealing Espionage is Equal to Treason" was still there, but several other notices were added by it, some of them were colorful. They were about dance contests or painting contests. The illustrations on the other posters reduced the threat of the blood-red characters. Chun-Hui decided to ignore it. She had decided, after the nightmare she had during the previous night, that reporting Uncle Huang was not her duty because even though she had seen him before, her knowledge of him wouldn't help to know Uncle Huang's whereabouts now. If Uncle Huang turned up again to drink with her father, she might consider reporting him, especially if he smoked too much. The cigarette smoke was really annoying.

Would Mom report Uncle Huang if she had seen the poster? Mom might consult with Dad, but Dad wasn't at home. Would Chun-Hui's decision not to report Uncle Huang result in an invasion by the Communist soldiers? She really couldn't think too much. The foremost thing she should do was to be practical and make up the homework that she failed to complete the previous night.

Dad did not return home in the following days,

thus Uncle Huang did not visit. Mom's spirit was low, probably because Dad was not around and she had to do everything. Chun-Hui and her brother went to school as usual, and she maintained her unnoticed status as usual. One day after school, she saw two policemen standing in front of her home, talking to her mom.

"I don't have his address." Mom said. And one of the policemen spoke in a low voice.

"He called once when he arrived there, that was all. He did not call again." Mom replied. Another policeman said something.

"I told you, I don't know anything." Mom said. The two policemen wrote something on a notepad, but did not seem to be leaving. Chun-Hui felt it was safer not to be seen at this moment, she turned and stepped down the stairs. She'd go somewhere else first.

It was March, but the weather did not show any sign of spring. Showers of cold rain washed away the energy of shoppers, storekeepers dozed off behind the counter, and street vendors played cards or read tabloids by their goods that were covered by plastic sheets protecting them from rain. The streets were bleak, Chun-Hui walked toward the small park, she decided to wait fifteen minutes and then go home. The policemen wouldn't hang on that long.

In the park she saw that the seats of the swings were too wet to sit on, so she walked to another side of the park and surprisingly saw her brother was there, too. Was he also waiting for the departure of the two policemen? Chun-Hui weighed whether she should say hello to her brother and sit beside him to wait together. In that case she would have to talk about their dad who had not been in touch for days, according to what she had overheard of Mom's conversation with the two policemen. And Uncle Huang, who was on the posters everywhere… Chun-Hui did not feel she had the mood to talk about it with her brother, so she walked away and sat down on a porch of a closed store, where she could see her brother's profile. "I can take action after him", she thought to herself.

Chun-Hui's brother Chun-Shih was two years older than she, although they went to the same elementary school, they did not have a lot to share.

Chun-Hui felt that her brother was closer to Mom than she was, because Chun-Shih could share Mom's thoughts. Chun-Hui was always absent-minded, no opinion and no sense of responsibility. Chun-Hui wondered whether or not the reason that Chun-Shih was in the park instead of at home was the same to hers. Was it a better decision that they stayed away when their mother was interrogated by the police?

Did Chun-Shih know the man on the posters was Uncle Huang? If so, would he report it to the police? Did Mom recognize the man was Uncle Huang? If so, would Mom report it to the police? What would happen to them if they recognize Uncle Huang and did not report it?

Earlier in school, Chun-Hui's unfinished home-work had gotten her busted. She had hoped to get away, but she calculated it wrong. She got away with unfinished homework more than once, because the teachers had too much homeworks to grade, they sometimes only checked the first one or two pages of the homework presented on each child's desk. Today Chun-Hui was hit by the teacher's bamboo stick three times as punishment, and was bade to make it up during the recesses. Later Chun-Hui realized she could have gotten away had Cheng Mei-Ru not reported on her. Chun-Hui was very surprised that Cheng Mei-Ru would have done this to her. First because Chun-Hui was not like those troublemakers who were often reported to the teachers. Second, Cheng Mei-Ru never was the kind of girl reporting on classmates. It was understandable if Cheng Mei-Ru was given a hard time or bullied that she took actions of revenge or self-defence, but Chun-Hui's not having finished her homework was not Cheng Mei-Ru's business at all.

Ever since that day, Chun-Hui was reported by Cheng Mei-Ru on a regular basis. At first Chun-Hui was really annoyed, then the incidents at home had left her exhausted. Mom decided to take Chun-Shih and Chun-Hui to resettle in the countryside. Packing and moving tired them, so Chun-Hui completely gave up her studies. Knowing she was leaving, Chun Hui's teachers no longer cared about her performance in school.

Chun-Shih and Chun-Hui's father never returned home. Chun-Hui did not ask Mom, those days she was easily irritated, or depressed, or absent-minded. They threw away a lot of their stuff during their move, Chun-Hui remembered she felt most pity for a brand new book in a foreign language, on its cover was a young man of black skin and big smile. The only words on the cover she could recognize were 1971. The place they were living was much smaller, Chun-Hui shared the same bedroom with Mom, and they put up a partition with closets and shelves by the living quarters so that Chun-Shih could have his own bedroom. There was no room for Dad, but soon enough Chun-Hui realized where Dad was and why they did not need to have room for him.

Chun-Shih and Chun-Hui transferred to a smaller school. Chun-Hui was happy that the homework assigned by the teachers at the new school was much lighter and much easier. She maintained her style of not standing out, not being noticed. Chun-Shih had been more active in their former school, but he was much quieter since they moved.

Several months later, one day Mom told them they were going to visit Dad. The three of them got up early and took several bus rides to a place with high gray walls and barb wire. A booth was at the top where two walls met, someone was in the booth, watching.

Dad was imprisoned. Chun-Hui finally realized it. That was why they had to move to a smaller place, and that was why they did not have to save a place for Dad. After the check-in line, they entered a hall with large tables, similar to the common dining room in Chun-Hui's former school, only the windows here were much higher, they couldn't look out. All the men wore baggy uniforms of faded blue. Chun-Hui did not recognize Dad until one man stood up and walked toward them. Chun-Hui thought her parents might hug, but they did not. All of them found a place and sat down. They exchanged some words like old neighbors chatting. There was no point at all to the conversation.

Chun-Hui couldn't help but glance at the other tables, those visiting families and their incarcerated husbands, fathers, brothers, or sons. Why were they here? And why was Dad here? Chun-Hui's parents cared very much about explaining things to their children, even before they raised questions. And when they did not explain certain things, they knew it was because they thought it was not their business, or beyond their understanding.

Chun-Hui felt ill at ease, she did not know how to participate in her family's conversation. Dad seemed to have lost some weight, she wanted to look at him more closely but also felt embarrassed to look at him. Chun-Hui felt the tension in Mom gradually loosened, her hand held her husband's hand, although their topics were still about insignificant matters, like the weather, the food they ate, and the plants around their new homes.

After a certain time Chun-Hui did not know how long, a male voice broadcasting something, and all the people began to stand up and leave. This time Chun-Hui's parents hugged, they hugged for a long time. Then Dad hugged Chun-Shih and Chun-Hui, he bade them, "Support your mother."

On their bus rides home, Dad's words hummed in Chun-Hui's ears. "Support your mother." Dad never talked like the parents of her classmates who emphasized "obedience" all the time. "Support" was definitely a new vocabulary for her, which made her feel like she was older than she really was.

The following years, Mom would pay Dad visits from time to time. Sometimes they went with her, sometimes Mom left them at home. In the first years, Mom's become very irritable before her visit, and much easier after the visit, until her trips to the penitentiary became routine.

*

Chun-Hui received an email inquiring about her experience after her father was incarcerated. It was from an art curator, who was also a daughter of a political prisoner in the 1960s. Dad had passed away the sixth year after he was released. That time Chun-Shih was in America, he had settled down there after completing his graduate degree of information technology. When he returned to Taiwan for their father's funeral, Chun-Hui proved something that had been hidden in her mind for decades: Chun-Shih blamed Dad for his irresponsible actions against the government and the consequences they had to endure. For all the nineteen years of Dad's incarceration, Mom,

Chun-Shih and Chun-Hui had been harrassed by police from time to time. Chun-Hui's performance in school was mediocre, but Chun-Shih was an excellent student in every subject. To his regret, each time he was applying for an award or a scholarship, he'd been cut off for unspoken reasons. Even when he was going to graduate school in the US, he had to overcome a lot of troubles that his peers never came up against.

Being asked about her experience, the first thought Chun-Hui has in mind was Chun-Shih. How much more he would have accomplished had their father not been a dissident and a political prisoner? But, was it fair to have such an assumption?

Chun-Hui never talked about it with Chun-Shih. She had assumed that Chun-Shih wouldn't want to talk about it. Or, it was she who avoided talking about it.

Chun-Hui inquired more about the art events the curator was working on, and the reason why she was interviewed. The reply came back quickly, explaining it was to document the experience of the families of White Terror victims. The art curator sent several files about herself, her projects, and related reports of White Terror. It was the first time Chun-Hui learned the term "White Terror" and she immediately could feel it. The invisible threat she and her mother and brother had lived within for nearly two decades. Chun-Hui decided not to respond to the email anymore, she wished she never had responded to it in the first place. She deleted the email, not wanting to be upset by the ghostly past.

About ten days later, the art curator emailed Chun-Hui again. She said she understood that many victims and their families did not want to talk about the past, and if Chun-Hui was interested in reading the interviews of others, she'd email her. Chun-Hui did not reply, and she did not delete the email, either.

Chun-Hui was a mother of two children now, her son was a college freshman, her daughter was in high school. Her son was a quiet boy like her, but her daughter was very active in school activities. She published articles in student journals, participated in debating teams, and ran as a student body representative. Chun-Hui's mother once commented that an eloquent and opinionated girl in her time certainly would be put in jail. Chun-Hui was shocked when hearing it, but wasn't it true? Looking back, her daughter did inherit many traits of her father. Before her father was imprisoned, he was an excellent speaker, a strong thinker, and a charming activist.

"Mom, I bought some taro at a good price in the late-afternoon market. Do you want some? I can bring it to you now." Chun-Hui called her mother, who lived by herself two blocks away.

"Don't bother. Make something for your children."

"I did. I bought more than we can consume, the vendor was about to leave when I went to him, and he gave me all the taro left." Chun-Hui felt she was eager to see her mother now, but she needed some excuse.

Chun-Hui and Mom peeled the taro, washed them, and put them in the soup made of pig bones Mom had prepared before Chun-Hui arrived. As the soup was cooking on mild fire, they took a break. Chun-Hui finally spoke out, "Mom, an artist is asking me about Dad. They are organizing art events about political prisoners in the past." Chun-Hui figured Mom wouldn't know the term curator, she simply said an "artist". Mom did not seem to be surprised. She told Chun-Hui the government was talking about rectifying the past injustice, she also got information from some agencies.

"Do you think Dad should have avoided becoming involved in something that could end in incarceration?" Chun-Hui raised the question that she had no idea did it constitute an answerable question or not. Or, was it appropriate to ask such a question at all?

"It had been very difficult the first years your dad was in jail, not only was the role of the husband and the father gone, but there were also the deliberate insults and harassment from the authorities. At first I thought your dad was reckless participating in those gatherings against the government, but having witnessed how terrible it could be to the people, I realized that there was just no way your dad and his friends could stay silent about it. If we backed down, those villains would have no limit to their evil."

Throughout her school life, Chun-Hui always told

her classmates and friends that her father was working in a military camp, and, because his work was quite sensitive, he couldn't go home. From time to time, they went to visit him. It was a scenario Chun-Hui made up according to the fragments of conversations her mother had with others she eavesdropped on. She knew having a version of her story consistent with her mother's was the safest thing to do, although the mother and the daughter never discussed about coordinating their stories. What was the story Chun-Shih told? Chun-Hui would never know. It was not a topic between herself and her brother. Did Mom ever discuss it with Chun-Shih? Chun-Hui did not feel she really wanted to know.

After his release, Dad tried to write down what he kept in his mind over the years. That was what he and Uncle Huang were trying to do—spreading the idealism of socialism, something that certainly was a taboo in the past. All the papers, journals and reference books, among other publications they had used were burned by Mom right after his disappearance. Chun-Hui recalled the young black author's big smile on the cover of the poetry back a long time ago. Later in the library of her college, she found the same book and the title she had been too young to recognize: *My Name is Afrika.* To Dad, trying to recall what he memorized in his mind long ago was a challenge, but after two decades, he was told that these topics were outdated, the camp of socialist countries had collapsed or become markets for capitalism.

"It is a different matter." Father tried to explain, but he seemed to be living in a different time and got confused as well.

"I should have let your dad know that I eventually understood his political decisions, but I did not. Having had to change jobs, transfer you and your brother to another school, hide everything we had and live like criminals made me unwilling to support your dad. And my bitterness only made your dad unforgivable to you and your brother."

"I was all right." Chun-Hui did not know how to comfort her mother. Throughout her childhood and teenage years, even she did not directly suspect the threats from the law enforcement or the watching eyes from their neighbors, teachers, or co-workers, she could feel the fears of her mother and brother.

There was a time, the three of them crowded in the only bedroom at night, any sound, wind gusts, or tree rustling, or frog croaks could frighten them easily. Even today, Chun-Hui needed the music of streaming water to help her fall asleep. Not to calm down her mind like meditators used it, but to engage her ears.

The light of the setting sun filtered into the living room, to the old chair Father had occupied often before his passing. It had been a second-hand piece of furniture when they acquired it, and the long sitting of Chun-Hui's father during the six years from his release from prison to his death had left a sunken area on the green seat of artificial leather. They had moved to a small apartment closer to the town, so they had better access to the public transportation. During the six years, most of the trips her parents made were to the hospital.

What was in his mind during the moments he sat there with his eyes casting in blankness all the time? Chun-Hui felt she had betrayed her father, as well as her mother and brother by not knowing more about their past. She had dodged the difficulties they had shared. Had she been more sensitive and more brave, she might have the opportunity to provide support to her unfortunate father.

Her father was never a traitor of the country as the charge resulting in his confinement claimed, but Chun-Hui felt she was the traitor of her father.

Chun-Hui sat down on the chair, looked around, trying hard to imagine what Father had seen during the time before his passing.

Green Island General Hospital

If a dictator is going to tighten control, eliminate dissident voices, and silence public opinions, the most effective way is to persecute elites. In the recent history of Taiwan, the most politically active elites are medical physicians who have been trained by western medicine and are the most respected professionals in Taiwan's society. Their maxim, "Treat Diseases and Heal the World" explained the missions that medical physicians are expected to conduct. And in the 1950s, right after the Nationalist Party's defeat in China and retreat to Taiwan, doctors were the most outspoken groups to openly urge government reform.

Since 1951, the prison in Green Island, a small island of 17 Square KM in area and 33KM from southern Taiwan, began to take in doctors convicted on the charge of sedition. They were sentenced to from 15 to 25 years, and the evidence of their crimes were the publications about socialism they read, and meetings they had attended regarding their demand for a corruption-free government. They were moved there because the worst criminals and the most rebellious offenders should be isolated from the society. Even though their sentences of imprisonment were so long, at least their lives were spared. Under the draconian Martial Law, many of their colleagues were sentenced to death, had they been found to be members of certain leftist organizations.

Political prisoners in Green Island were forced to labor, for the authorities believed that laboring was the best way to "correct" one's ideas. In the windy island, there were not many crops to grow, so these doctors were assigned to the roughly built Health Office for the military officers stationed in the island and their employees. They also helped the inmates and the small population of native people. Through the military system, the dominant power under the Martial Law, they could order medication and medical devices to be shipped to Green Island fast enough for their practice. Gradually they established a hospital of 30 beds, and with a simply equipped but clean and safe operation room.

From 1951 to 1960, among around one thousand prisoners, there were as many as fourteen medical physicians incarcerated in Green Island. Most of them were in their thirties and their professions covered ophthalmology, internal medicine, dentistry, otolaryngology, dermatology, surgery, immunology, and obstetrics and gynecology. There was also an expert of bacteriology and an expert of disease control. It was a time when Green Island had the highest doctor-population ratio throughout Taiwan, and probably the whole world.

Because they were working outside the buildings of the prison, they had more free time for themselves. From time to time they'd receive medical publications their families mailed to them after the troublesome procedure of censorship. They studied together and discussed in their informal seminars. Yen Shueh-Hung was the youngest among all these doctors, in fact, he was arrested before he could complete his residency. After several years in Green Island, Shueh-Hung felt that he might have learned more from these seniors than he had in medical school.

Green Island was warm all year, when there were

no patients, Shueh-Hung liked to swim in the ocean. He liked to swim to an islet about 1KM from Green Island and return. He called the islet Ghost Islet. The several moments he spent on the rocky Ghost Islet made him feel he was no longer confined, he was a free man. Sometimes Dr. Su Yeh-Peng, the otolaryngologist, would join him. Looking back at Green Island from the Ghost Islet, one can see the extraordinary landscape shaped by lava and coral reefs. Minerals contained in the lava thousands of years ago still glimmered over the rocky cliffs, white flowers of reef pemphis and purple flowers of bayhops decorated the shoreline, balancing the wild scenes of the screw pines.

Sometimes Shueh-Hung considered he would swim toward another direction, to the borderless ocean, until he was exhausted, and he would never return. He would never return to the endless incarceration and this hopeless life.

Sergeant Ko, the supervisor of the prison, prohibited them from swimming. He provided no reason when Shueh-Hung objected, "We won't escape, there is no place to escape from here anyway." He swam as he could, behind the watch of Sergeant Ko, sometimes he swam in the night, risking his life in the unseen and unpredictable undercurrents.

Sergeant Ko was a very mean man, Shueh-Hung suspected that he secretly enjoyed abusing the inmates, especially these doctors, out of his jealousy of their teamship and shame about his own education. He'd cancel their hours of outdoor activities, or confiscate their books, or make them stand under the scorching sun for a long time with excuses of very trivial affairs. Shueh-Hung had been put in the solitary room twice by Ko as the consequence of his confrontation. Sometimes in the morning roll call rally, his inmates would restrain Shueh-Hung from protesting against Sergeant Ko, in case not only Shueh-Hung, but all of them might be punished without justified cause.

But as if they were avenged by heaven, Sergeant Ko fell ill. He was seen holding his chest from time to time, like he was about to vomit. But so far no doctor had been consulted by Sargeant Ko. Understandably he was too proud to consult with these criminals, although they had successfully treated many patients, including a case of appendicitis, a case of acute gastric ulcer, several cases of typhoid fever, several cases of trachoma, many cases of intestinal parasites and many cases of tooth cavities. They even had delivered two babies for local women.

Shueh-Hung never saw Ko show illness in front of him, and he knew even if he did, he would not have any sympathy for Ko. Dr. Hsu Jiang-Sheng, the internist, said Sergeant Ko's wife had asked him in private, and he thought Ko's syndromes were more likely caused by gallstones, but the heartburn made them suspect it was a heart disease.

"Did you tell her?" Shueh-Hung inquired.

"No, I can't make a diagnosis without checking the patient in person."

Later they heard that Sergeant Ko had booked the ship back to Taitung for treatment. They felt funny. Taitung was the remotest county with least medical resources in Taiwan, had Ko decided to take treatments in Green Island, he certainly could get better treatment in their hospital. But they said nothing. That was Sergeant Ko's decision, out of his arrogance and his contempt of these doctors violating his political belief and loyalty.

But on the day Sergeant Ko's ship was scheduled to bound for Taiwan, Green Island was hit by a huge storm. Torrential rain and gusty wind seemed to tear apart and sink the entire island. Of course the ship trip was canceled. Shueh-Hung was pleased, he was convinced it was god's deed to seek justice for them, although it was still far away from the rectification they deserved. The storm was so powerful, it was expected that the transportation between Green Island and Taiwan would have to be postponed for at least one week.

"Will Sergeant Ko consider to be treated here if his pain turns really bad during this week?" Dr. Lin Shu-Kui asked, he was a surgeon.

"He will have no choice, right?" ophthalmologist Dr. Hu Chih-Lin said.

"Then let us kill him on the operation table!" Shueh-Hung shouted in an agitated tone. All the other doctors turned their head to look at him.

"We are healthcare providers, we don't kill patients" Dr. Lin responded after a moment.

"Look!" Shueh-Hung opened his white robe to show the faded green prison uniform under the robe, "We are not doctors. To the eye of Sergeant Ko and all the people working here, we are criminals, we are the national traitors who should be punished, reeducated and corrected! We are not doctors, we are prisoners! Nothing but prisoners!"

They all fell silent. It was true, no matter how hard these physicians and scientists wished to forget about their real status in Green Island, their lives and careers had been stained, no matter whether they had seditious ideas against the nation or not.

With an effort to relieve the heavy ambiance, Dr. Su Yeh-Peng proposed, "Let's open his chest and then tell him, oops, the cardiologist is not with us!" All of them laughed, but only for a moment. The cardiologist they all had in mind was Dr. Kuo Lian-Tsong, who had been executed before they were transported to Green Island. When Taiwan was under the Japanese colonial rule, Kuo Lian-Tsong already began his campaign for self-governance as a student activist in medical school. And after the Nationalist Party took over Taiwan, he campaigned for the independence of Taiwan beside his medical practice in the teaching hospital affiliated with the National Taiwan University. It was the greatest taboo of the totalitarian ruler. Kuo nevertheless organized several events to increase the awareness of self-governance and local Taiwanese cultural identity that was repressed by the Chinese identity.

Active as he was for his political idealism, Dr. Kuo Lian-Tsong was a top cardiologist in Taiwan. When the society was suffering from political commotions, he had used all his means to get information of the fast development in cardiology from the US to make up the insufficiency of diagnosing rheumatic heart disease, a fatal health threat unusually common in Taiwan, with a tool as simple as stethoscope that was almost the only thing available in Taiwan at that time. When the electrocardiogram was finally introduced to Taiwan, Dr. Kuo lectured as often as possible to teach his fellow doctors how to make diagnoses with this fancy technology. They all believed that the death of Dr. Kuo Lian-Tzong had unjustly slowed down the progress of heart disease treatment in Taiwan.

Sheuh-Hung wiped his tears quietly.

That night Sheuh-Hung was woken up by a gunshot. When he opened his eyes, he realized it was a huge thunderbolt. He couldn't forget the fears he had for himself and his colleagues during their trials. What is the point for them to spend so much energy treating patients, and the regime kills hundreds of them without mercy? Sheuh-Hung thought in despair. The night was lit by flashes of lightning strikes, he couldn't sleep again, and he knew he wasn't the only one awake.

Several days later he ran into Sergeant Ko in front of the Health Office when he was bringing some medical supplies from the office for disinfection. On good days they made use of ultraviolet rays in the sunlight to help with disinfection. The storm had mostly died down, but the ship transportation between Green Island and Taiwan was not resumed yet. Sergeant Ko looked languid, but he was all right.

With his habitual manner of disdain, Sergeant

Ko commented, like he was completely aware of how he was hated, "Don't think you can murder me. I will never give you the chance." Slowly Sheuh-Hung turned his head to Ko, and replied him word by word in a determined tone, "No. We are not going to murder you. Our profession is too noble to do harm to any patient on purpose."

"Why not?" Sergeant Ko sneered, "You have thought about it all the time since I got ill, haven't you?"

Sheuh-Hung looked at the expansive ocean behind Ko, and the Ghost Islet on the right. The sky was turning bright, clouds were thinning out, and beams of sunlight gradually emerged from the growing blueness. The tumultuous waves on the ocean were smoothing now, although it took a long time. He turned his face to Sergeant Ko again and looked straight in his eyes, "Because we don't want to be like you, Sergeant Ko."

With his medical supplies in hands, Sheuh-Hung walked past Ko. Today he might try to swim again.

Read Between The Lines

Dear Son:

How is everything going in school?

You might be under surveillance, my child

Together with this letter, I mail you several books I've finished reading

These publications have passed censorship

I believe that masterpieces by western writers can teach you about life

Works by local writers are often banned

I want to remind you to practice your oration every-day and pronounce each word correctly

Let people think you are urbane, not raised in a rural area

Exercise regularly

So you won't attend forbidden gatherings of activ-ists

Go to bed on time, good sleep is very important to

your health
      Do not risk hanging out after curfew
Be an independent person
      Be cautious making new acquaintances
and solve problems in your studies by yourself as
much as possible
      helpers could try to absorb you into underground
political organizations
Be a law-abiding student, and focus on your study
      Do not get involved in political affairs in case you
get in trouble

Your uncle Chung wrote to ask after you
      His letter was mailed from the prison on a remote
island
Write him back when you have time
      For his soul and body are tortured
Tell him about the progress you have made in college
      But do not complain about how your activities are
restrained on campus

Our small eatery is okay
      after bribering the local police

And we sell our food at the street market, too
    through a deal with a gang

Your grandaunt has passed away in the US
    As a dissident she couldn't return to her homeland
She is buried in the county cemetery called Rose
Garden
    Just like she was a thorny flower who never gave in
May she rest in peace
    She died with anger and regret

A water vendor set up a new stall in town
    *Running water is so polluted, there is no way we
can drink it*
Our food tastes better after cooking with clean water
    *We no longer need to add a lot of spices to cover
up foul smells from the muddy water*

My dear child, we have great hope in you
    We are so worried about you
You are trained to be an able man with a high education
    You will be brainwashed with propaganda
One day you will serve your country with your profession

You will be working like a machine
You will have a prosperous life
　You will be impoverished in spirit
A hardworking man, a model citizen
　An obedient person, but living safely

Love, Dad

A Terrible Beauty Is Born

From the speaker on the ceiling, a coarse voice broadcasted, "Yang San-Jih, you have a visitor!" The voice was impatient, and he knew why. His visitor was the lawyer Yuo Ching-Shui, who had volunteered to defend him. It had only been two days since the hard-working lawyer had last visited, and the prison administration saw him as a nuisance because every time Yuo came he questioned them about the rights of the imprisoned. He liked to quote, "The regime of the institution should seek to minimize any differences between prison life and life at liberty which tend to lessen the responsibility or the respect due to the prisoners as human beings." He would add, "Standard Minimum Rules for the Treatment of Prisoners, United Nations, 1957." The year 1957 sounded piercing in the ear because 23 years later, the administration of the prison still seemed completely ignorant of the rules. In the minds of the staff, prisoners should be tortured and condemned for what they had done. "Respect" for these thugs? That was a radical idea.

The meeting room was one of the arraignment rooms with a rusted iron desk, several dusty folding chairs and unused file cabinets. The paint on the walls was peeling, and rain water must have dripped from the high windows for years, leaving layers of dirty marks on the mottled walls. This prison had been the telecommunications lab during the Japanese colonial period, and now its space was altered awkwardly to incarcerate people. Yang had been here only a few weeks, and from other inmates he learned it could be as hot as hell in summer. The added walls and blocked windows had stopped the flow of air, and the odor of sweating men mixed with the smells of urine from the poorly installed toilets and plumbing was truly torturous.

Isn't being confined sufficient punishment? Yang wondered. No matter what evils one had done, they were already punished by being deprived of their freedom for extended periods. Yang had no idea why anyone of his inmates was here. He never asked, and no one asked him. If anyone ever did ask this question of him, what would he answer? Should he say he tried to overturn the government? Would they understand?

Yang San-Jih hurried to the meeting room. He carried pages of papers which he had filled with words for his own defense during the two days since their last meeting:

"The status of Taiwan as an independent entity should be open to public debate. No information about this issue should be hidden from the population in order to mislead public opinion. No opinions should be oppressed."

"Freedom of speech must be restored. All bans over the issuance of certain publications, the establishment of new news media, and the organization of new political groups, should be lifted."

"People advocating free speech, including open debates regarding Taiwan's independence, should not be criminalized."

"With uncompromised freedom of speech and expression, when naming civic groups or organizations, there shall be an option of using 'Taiwanese' in the name instead of 'Chinese.' For example, Taiwanese Writers Association v.s Chinese Writers Association"

There was a lot more within the pages, but his lawyer suggested, "Perhaps we shouldn't mention the independence of Taiwan at this moment, but just say the 'status of Taiwan'..." Then he put down Yang's papers, and said in a low voice with an unclear message as to whether he was bringing good news or bad news, "They might not charge you with sedition."

"What does that mean?"

"They might charge you with a much lighter crime, such as 'Violation of Social Orders with Violence.'"

"And what does that mean?" Yang asked again.

"No military trial, just a criminal trial for general crimes."

Complicated feelings soared in Yang's mind. Since his arrest during the protest of Formosa Magazine, he had been preparing to die. He wrote his statements eagerly and restlessly, day and night, like a dying man. Whenever thoughts occurred, he took out his pen and paper and wrote them down desperately. And in the night he wrote and rewrote his letters to his wife and daughter, apologizing for having created hassles for them with the police instead of taking care of them. He wished his death could finally put an end to their troubles, but he knew, based on the experiences of his martyred comrades, that the harassment of their families never stopped.

Now came the news of no military trial, which meant that the ruling party was very likely to spare his life, although he still could be sentenced to a lifetime in jail. He did not know what to think now.

"But why?"

"It's said that America has pressed the government a lot."

"Great, we've been heard by the international society finally." Yang was agitated. After all these years, all the fights and horrors, sacrifices and losses, they had actually achieved something, although there was still a long way to go.

"No military trials at all?" He couldn't believe it.

"Some of the editors will still be tried by court-martial, but the US has sent a human rights watch group to attend the trials."

"Who will be tried by court-martial, do you know?" Yang was worried.

"Shih Ming-De, Huang Hsin-Chieh, Chen Ju, Lu Shu-Liang… I guess… they are the core members of the alleged insurgency."

Thinking that his friends might die and he might not, Yang's mood turned heavy. He had been preparing for his own death. It had never dawned on him that some of them might escape death, and some of them might not.

His lawyer patted his shoulder, "We will have a different defending strategy soon. Take care. Oh, and I assume this is good news for your family; remember to write them."

Yang got up on his feet and slowly walked back to his cell, still not clear what to think about this new turn of events. In the corridor four inmates were moving wood panels under the supervision of a guard. For weeks they had been tearing down existing window shades left from the old times and installing ugly panels that looked like concrete molds abandoned in construction sites. They nailed the panels over the window frames, blocking the last bit of air and light in the corridor. Why? After staying in this place for weeks, Yang began to realize that there were a lot of tasks aimed at making this world worse, not better. And people taking on these tasks probably were not aware of it. But why did they do it? Did they take orders from their superiors without questioning the reason, or they were deceived by causes they believed to be great? Justice, for example? What justice is there in depriving prisoners of a decent environment with air and light? But the condemned are not entitled to claim their rights.

***

Since Yang San-Jih's arrest, Chiang Sung-Nien had nothing to write for his report on him. He had hoped Yang could get away, but after watching him for nearly 20 years, he knew better than anyone that Yang certainly would not stand aside. In fact, he was more deeply involved than the authorities realized, but Chiang respected and admired Yang too much to bring himself to report every detail of his activities.

Since Yang's guilt would be decided by the court anyway, should Chiang come to a conclusion about Yang in his final report? Chiang didn't feel he could conclude his report. He felt there was still a lot he wanted to write; not only about Yang's activities, but also Yang's literary works.

Chiang decided to continue writing. After all, he knew no one was really checking his reports. The authorities had become a machine that didn't care how you filled in your files, only that you turned your files in on time. He had come to realize that the loyalty the government asked for did not come from ideas, but from the absence of ideas. People were engaged by routines and never bothered to consider the reasons for the routines. One time his son got quite ill and he had to run between his work, home and hospital and really couldn't squeeze in any time to watch Yang and write up-to-date reports, so he simply repeated what he had written several years ago. No one gave him a hard time for copying himself, because neither report had been read.

Nonetheless, Chiang wrote diligently. Sometimes he wrote even more than Yang did. He developed into a certain kind of writer himself. Chiang knew that, having observed a writer like Yang and having read through all Yang's literary works, he had developed a deeper perspective as a writer. His reports became more focused on his research, which he conducted for himself, not for the authorities.

Chiang reasoned that continuing to write about Yang would give him the opportunity to write more about his literature. He opened his notebook and wrote:

> *Resistance is the central theme of Yang's latest collection of essays Wishes of Workers, and his collections of short stories Under the Factory Chimney and Factory Man. Wishes of Workers was published in late June(1979), and both Under the Factory Chimney and Factory Man were published in 1975. In each of these three publications, Yang dealt with issues regarding the laborers' self-awareness and self-esteem, as well as the conditions of the*

workplace. These were also recurring themes in Yang's earlier works.

These three publications thus pursue more active measures to improve the workers' situation, including founding unions and demanding participation in factory management.

Should I quote Yang? Chiang asked himself. He felt a little self-conscious that over all these years, his reports had become more and more like academic papers. In his previous reports, he had compared Yang's works to those of John Steinbeck and Upton Sinclair, and now ideas about how a fiction writer expresses his activism spinned in his mind. He read a paragraph in the <u>Wishes of Workers</u> about the difficulty of creating a union for workers, "Our boss prevents the establishment of a union. Once a person mentions any possibility of a union, he or she certainly will be fired or turned in to law enforcement with accusations of inappropriate behavior... even if a union is established, the heads of the union will be paid off by the business owners in order to interfere in the union's elections..."

Threats on individuals' lives make collective defiance impossible. However, when the repression increases to the point of being intolerable, workers with little to lose will connect, first secretly then openly, to strike back.

To deal with emerging resistance, the business owners typically separate workers into different classes. The workers that believe they are enjoying some degree of privilege will become the repressors of workers at the bottom. Unfortunately, the chance that collective action will be taken by workers at the bottom is meager since they hardly have the time, resources, or training to put together any kind of organized protest.

In <u>Under the Factory Chimney,</u> Yang introduced the fact that the right to strike is granted to workers in the UK and the US, especially when they are deprived of holidays or break time, or their wages are reduced. Solidarity is the precondition for workers to negotiate with their employers, but it is a difficult goal to achieve. The tricks of employers have been *applied throughout history again and again, and they have always worked. It seems that the more severe the discipline that is imposed on workers, the more unlikely it is that they will be able to cultivate self-awareness. Like the fruit pickers in John Steinbeck's novels, they don't feel the urge to take any action until their working conditions severely worsen to an impossible situation. Thus, Yang raises a question in his fiction that must have been raised by many labor rights activists throughout history: how does restriction of choice narrow one's sense of justice?*

That's long enough for a weekly report, Chiang told himself. He knew he had more to write, but he might wait for next week.

***

Yang lay on his bunk bed, and his brain was blank. That rarely happened. He always had all kinds of thoughts in his mind. Now he felt trapped. For the first time in his life he realized how the operation of a system can trap one's ideas. He felt muffled, suffocated.

There were small windows above their bunk beds, and he could feel the changes of light during the day by observing the little bit of sky he was able to see. He wished to see trees, to hear the rustling of leaves. Were there trees around their prison? The stillness in the air was man-made. The lifelessness must be the result of a certain kind of pleasure for the torturers that he couldn't understand.

He had written down his defense, page after page, by introducing the Home Rule of Ireland in the late 19th century. Home Rule demanded autonomy for Ireland, such as self-governance by establishing a local parliament. Presently Taiwan was not only ruled by a political party from the mainland but also a parliament with representatives elected in the mainland. It was very odd to have representatives from other provinces in China deciding affairs that happened only in Taiwan. Additionally, without any means for the Taiwanese people to have reelections in China, these people had been in their positions forever. Over the past three decades, they had become senile and outdated, making decisions based on the false illusion that they could rule a territory that was inaccessible to them.

Yang continued to write, "To disillusion them, the only way is to have a Taiwan-centered political body. Playing down the fact that mainland China is no longer under the control of the Nationalist Party is to ignore the greatest interests of the population that actually is under the rule of the Nationalist Party. "

"For example, Mandarin is not the most used language in Taiwan, but Taiwanese dialects are not allowed in many circumstances, including school classrooms. The beauty of the local culture that is most intimate to the public, such as folk tales, folk music, and other folk art, is lost."

"A Taiwan-centered political body doesn't require the expulsion of Mandarin and everything from China. It means first, to preserve local cultural assets, such as architecture, art, and rituals; second, to reconnect the people's bond with the land through local agriculture; third, to establish a system of self-governance by reactivating the general elections of regional representatives within Taiwan."

Self-governance, that was what Yang and his comrades wanted, and it absolutely was not too much to ask. How many of them would be put to death by a court-martial decision? Yang thought to himself. Their faces appeared in his head one by one, tearing at his heart. He had prepared to die for his idealism, but now he felt guilty, quilty to continue to live if some of them were to die.

Yang thought of the lines from the poem "Easter 1916" by William Yeats:

...Too long a sacrifice
Can make a stone of the heart.
O when may it suffice?
That is Heaven's part, our part
To murmur name upon name,
As a mother names her child
When sleep at last has come
On limbs that had run wild.
What is it but nightfall?
No, no, not night but death;
Was it needless death after all?...

It was late. Other than the occasional lights of the guards, his dim lamp was the only illumination in the entire prison. Yang was exhausted after thinking and writing restlessly for hours. And he realized that there were tears in his eyes, eyes which he could hardly keep open now. He recited Yeats' poem again and again before drifting into sleep.

In his dreams he found himself in a grassy swamp with his daughter. It had rained for days, and sunlight was finally emerging from the thinning clouds. He felt the wind. It was drying the grass as well as the leaves and trunks of trees that had swollen with too much moisture for the past few days. He stretched out his arms to catch the sunlight. He tried to hold his daughter's hand but she had already walked ahead by herself. She walked so far that he worried she might come upon snakes. He wanted to warn her but didn't want to scare her. He wanted her to see the other side of the swamp, but he also worried about the unknown risks ahead of her.

What was it like in Easter of 1916? He heard his daughter ask from a distance. She had crossed the weedy earth and was standing on a rock now. She turned and smiled at her father, waiting for an answer. What was it like in Easter of 1916?

***

He was wakened by a shriek cry, followed by someone's sobbing, then shouting and moaning from somewhere he couldn't locate. Since the windows were sealed, noises within the prison seemed louder, more distinct, and closer. There were various indications of commotion among the inmates from time to time, and Yang never had any idea what it was all about. He did not know the reasons why any of the men were here. Were they violent? Were they murderous? Were they mentally ill? Were they like him, innocent of the crimes they had been accused of committing? Were they actually victims rather than perpetrators? Some of them did look fierce or vulgar, and some of them seemed intimidated, probably because of those who looked fierce. Some of them exhibited a smooth cleverness from the streets, and others showed signs of retardation. . . But most of these men looked just like normal people one encounters daily outside of the prison.

It was barely past 5 o'clock, and Yang couldn't go back to sleep again. He couldn't wait to meet his lawyer. He decided to write more about his defense. At the same time he began to plot his new novel, a novel about his comrades who had tried all means of setting up a new political party but were not allowed. Thus they were all called the "Denied Partiers." He profiled each of his friends, especially those most likely to be tried by court-martial and sentenced to death. He knew writing was his redemption from the guilt of having escaped death.

When Yuo Ching-Shui finally came at around 9 o'clock, Yang pressed into his hands the 34 pages he had written during the past week. He noticed that the room looked shabbier than the last time they had met, and Yang gathered that it was because the windows on the corridor were blocked. The dust on the floor seemed to be thicker; the air felt heavier. Perhaps he should tell his lawyer that having sunlight and air was a human right, too. He'd bring it up after their discussion of his defense.

Yuo took a quick look at Yang's papers, and said, "San-Jih, you will be tried by 'Violation of Social Orders with Violence.' It's a relatively light charge, and the prosecutors will focus on violent actions you took during the demonstration. You won't need to argue about how Taiwan should be ruled and by whom."

Yang sat back and sank into his chair, speechless. He had not thought that being spared his life would deprive him of his chance to make a statement about the real cause of their demonstrations, their long battle, and their beliefs that they were ready to die for. He turned his head toward the blocked windows, and he saw that the peeling paint on the walls looked worse than ever.

Stolen Life, Stolen Story

Dear Louise:

I write this letter to congratulate your success of your short story "The Stolen Life"* published by the Independent Evening News on Mar 7.

I have to admit that when reading your story, I was infuriated. I had no doubt that you'd stolen my story. On January 22nd, I forgot my notebook at your place. The notebook contained hundreds of my notes for stories I planned to write. I wrote down my memories of the days when we met our fellow democracy campaigners, many of the notes were about how we had been trapped and arrested one-by-one by the fundamentally unjust legal system. I put down more notes after the meeting and before leaving your place, after we decided that I should never see you in pri-

------

Stolen Life (偷生) also means a very low and worthless life.

vate again. That afternoon I stopped by a library and a bookstore, and did a bit of shopping afterwards. When I went home, I realized I was without my notebook.

I thought I had left it in the library, so I went back to look for it. However, the notebook was not in the library, neither at where I had been sitting nor had it ended up at the Lost and Found office. So I visited the bookstore again, the bookstore keeper said he did not see anything like a notebook around. I went to the grocery store where I usually buy things, still my notebook was not found. I was in despair, and completely lost as far as my writing plans were concerned.

I had planned to write the story of my late friend Chiang Da, I wrote the beginning part based on my memory:

Grandpa Chiang's last words sounded like someone's curriculum vitae:
Du Ming-Hui, twenty-one years old
Stick Orderly
Tsungtou Community
Yuanlin Township

Graduate of the Tsiong-hua Agricultural High School

We stooped over to hear him, my younger sister even took a pen and papers to write it down, but she never figured out why these would be Grandpa Chiang's last words. After murmuring these words, Grandpa Chiang closed his eyes and stopped breathing, he was ninety-three years old.

While preparing for the funeral, we googled the name and the places that sounded like those last words he uttered by looking up possible combinations of Chinese characters which might fit, but did not find any clue relating Grandpa Chiang to the small place on the Chinese Mainland his dying words seemed to indicate. The 21-year-old Du Ming-Hui was lost in the mist of time. We searched the map of Grandpa Chiang's hometown in Hunan and found Yuanlin in Haui-hua, where there was an agricultural school. And the Tsungtou Community seemed to be an agricultural settlement, a place with about five hundred families. We also found there were some websites from China not available in Taiwan. Who was this Du Ming-Hui? Why was he in Grandpa

Chiang's mind during the last minutes in his life?

"To tell the truth, the place we found might not even be the place Grandpa Chiang was referring to. China is huge, and I did hear him say 'Tsiong-hua', not 'Huai-hua.'"

"True, and we have no idea how to write the characters that sound like 'Du Ming-Hui.' There might be hundreds of possible combinations." My sister said.

Grandpa Chiang's memorial service was held on a clear day in April. To our surprise, a lot more mourners than expected were in attendance. We had to borrow stools from the memorial service next to ours. Grandpa Chiang came to Taiwan with the military of the Nationalist Party, which was defeated by the Communist Party in 1949. He was discharged right after arriving in Taiwan, the military did not need so many soldiers, although the Nationalist government told people they were going to take back Mainland China as soon as the military was reconstructed and re-equipped. Sixty years had passed since that time, the political climates across the Taiwan Strait had changed so much. To people in Taiwan, Mainland

China was once a terrible enemy, then the largest and most enticing market in the world, then a terrible enemy again, and while remaining the most enticing market.

Grandpa Chiang moved to our neighborhood around twenty years ago, he rented a small place in an alley by himself. He was a quiet man and hardly had any visitors. In the first years he traveled occasionally, he'd leave home for several days but the neighbors never knew where he had gone and whom he had seen. We had no idea if Grandpa Chiang had family in Mainland China, and if so, whether he was in contact with them. If Grandpa Chiang had children, they certainly were much older than twenty-one years old. While preparing for Grandpa Chiang's funeral, we sorted his stuff and thought he might have married but his wife might have died or left him. We couldn't tell if he had children or not. After leaving the military, Grandpa Chiang had taken odd jobs here and there, he once made a living by driving a cab in Taipei. The most stable income he ever had made was during the years he worked as a guard for the warehouse of a furniture factory in the industrial park in Taoyuan. From a letter he wrote but did not mail, *we knew that Grandpa Chiang had a diploma from a teaching college in Shanghai. Since he had run from the war in such a hurry there was no way he could bring any paper that could prove he held a degree. In Taiwan, he couldn't find any way to restore his diploma. He had been told to attend college again but he needed to work all the time in order to sustain himself.*

While my sister and I were looking through Grandpa Chiang's belongings, which were worth no more than trash, his landlord stopped by to make sure all Grandpa Chiang's stuff was to be removed, so he could rent this place again. We admired his blunt attitude of zero empathy.

"He died in this house, will it bring bad luck to my property?"

"What are you talking about?" My sister was outraged, so I stood up and interposed.

"Mr. Huang, Grandpa Chiang lived to ninety-three years old and was taken back to heaven from this peaceful home, thanks to its good Feng-Shui. This

place is blessed."

Hearing this, Mr. Huang's face lit up. He gave us two weeks to move Grandpa Chiang's things, longer than we had expected, before he could rent the place again.

"The next tenant will have to pay higher rent for the good Feng-Shui, I bet." My sister said sarcastically.

Grandpa Chiang's last home was about the size of six tatamis. The only window looked out to nothing but the wall of another household. I suspected Grandpa Chiang's house was actually the back of a rowhouse, but cut into halves to lease separately. It was occupied by a single bed, a student desk, a cabinet and a shelf simply built of bricks and plywood panels. There were several books on the shelf, and a magnifying glass that Grandpa Chiang might have used for reading. We put Grandpa Chiang's official papers like his I.D., his certificate of retirement from the military and letters from his friends in a box. Most of the stuff would have to be thrown away. Did he have any relatives at all? Was he in contact with anyone in Taiwan or in China? A day calendar by the window was more than one year old, Grandpa Chiang probably no longer cared about time in his last days.

We wrote a simple obituary, and with our PC we made a simple layout similar to those we had seen before and printed fifty copies in a small xerox store across the street. We mailed them to people we found in a very old list of contacts that Grandpa Chiang must have written down many years ago.

Since the list of contacts was so old, we expected few would receive the mail, and even fewer would attend his memorial service. So when more than forty people arrived at Grandpa's funeral, we were hopeful to find more about Grandpa Chiang's personal history.

My sister tried to inquire of each guest how he or she was related to Grandpa Chiang with casual chatting, but most of the time it led her to completely irrelevant topics, like pets, food, traffic… When she tried to bring up more personal issues, sometimes her prying triggered alarm in the guest she was interviewing, other times her questions simply brought up endless gossip about people we didn't know at all.

Expecting fewer guests, we only prepared twenty handkerchiefs to those who provided funeral gifts, it was embarrassing. We must have looked desperate, because a lady in the service approached us and told us she might be able to help.*

"I have two athletic boys, they use many towels, so I always store about twenty new ones at home. I can call my sons and ask if they can bring them to me now."

"Thanks! Thanks!" I was going to grasp her hand to express my gratefulness, but thought I'd better bow to her instead.

The lady was called Vera, and her older son delivered twenty-five new towels in less than one hour by scooter. Vera told us Grandpa Chiang belonged to the same club for former residents of Zhejiang Province in Taiwan, she met him twice when attending their gatherings with her father years ago.

In traditional Taiwanese memorial service, mourners will bring a funeral gift, usually cash in a white envelope. The family of the deceased will return with a handkerchief or a towel, symbolically for them to wipe tears.

That was the first half of the story based on my efforts to recreate it from memory. Unfortunately my negligence in leaving my belongings somewhere I couldn't recall resulted in the postponement of my writing. When I read your story, I was first shocked, then angry. I have no doubt that my notebook was under your custody. Why didn't you return it to me? I was going to report you to the editors of the newspaper. I had no doubt that they would believe me, based on our long years of friendship and their knowledge about my writing background. Why didn't you develop your own scenarios instead of using mine?

At first I thought it was your revenge. In our open relationship of love or comradeship, there was always a competition that I did not want to admit. I knew you always wanted to be a writer, too, but I did not want to face it. The excuse I gave myself was you were engaged in raising your two children, and a writing career is not possible for a mother. I think my failure to acknowledge your wishes might have resulted in our break-up, for I did not want to confront you as a challenger. My eventual decision against calling the newspaper editors was for another reason though—honestly, after reading and re-reading your work, I think what you have achieved in this story is greater than mine, had I been the author of it.

In my story, the brother and sister eventually find that the 21-year-old Du Ming-Hui was a soldier killed during the Sino-Japanese War, who told Chiang Da to inform his parents about his death before his heart stopped beating. But as the Nationalist Troops were defeated by the Communist Army, Chiang Da was running for his life, he couldn't find a chance or a means to inform Du Ming-Hui's family about his death. Chiang Da eventually ended up in Taiwan, it was more unlikely to bring the news to Du Ming-Hui's family, for at that time any communication between China and Taiwan was completely cut off. But Chiang Da kept it in mind all his life, he never could put his promise to Du Ming-Hui aside. It was the only thing Grandpa Chiang couldn't let go even after more than seven decades had passed.

But in your story, without knowing my setting, you created a completely different plot. Chiang Da had been put in jail for painting graffiti on the wall of a factory that did not count his working hours and pay his wages honestly. The factory managers reported him and in order to get rid of him for good, they plotted to set him up by claiming he had intentionally damaged the statue of the national leader in an act of treason against the state. His vandalism charge ended up rolling into a charge of "attempting to subvert the government in the time of martial law." Chiang Da was detained in places he did not know, interrogated by people with titles or ranks he never heard of. Deprived of freedom and sleep, Chiang Da confessed, then recanted his confession, and confessed again. He had no idea why his protest of not being paid accordingly made him a national traitor. He had fought for the country and had to leave his parents and siblings because of his military career, now he was called a traitor? Hatred filled Chiang Da's mind, and after weeks of repetitive interrogation, the despair and fatigue finally made him give up hoping completely. He confessed everything and wished to be executed, but his blind confession did not constitute an offense deserving capital punishment quite yet.

That was why when he was temporarily locked in the same cell as Du Ming-Hui, who was sentenced to death for robbing arms from the prison guards and planning an insurgence for Taiwan's independence, Chiang Da proposed to die for him when they found the documents of their cases and identities were mistakenly switched by the prison.

Du Ming-Hui was surprised by Chiang Da's proposal, but Chiang Da said: "I have nothing to lose. You have family, you have dreams."

"As a veteran of the Nationalist Military, you are dying for a separatist?"

"I don't care about your separatism, I don't care if you guys want Taiwan to be independent or not. We shouldn't have come here. Taiwan should be left to Taiwanese people, and Taiwanese people should be left alone."

Chiang Da's proposal was rejected first, but he told Du Ming-Hui that he'd kill himself anyway, and Du Ming-Hui should never waste the chance to escape.

That's how Du Ming-Hui became Chiang Da and

was released after 4 years and 3 months imprisonment. But the freedom he had expected did not come. He realized he couldn't contact his family because all his family members were still under surveillance because of his crime. And as the former agitator Chiang Da, he was under surveillance as well. Being Chiang Da let Du Ming-Hui understand why Chiang Da had no motivation to live. He couldn't find a decent job, people seemed to distrust him as a mainlander in the first place, but when he tried to communicate with them in Taiwanese language, they were even more frightened.

He drifted in his own land as an outsider, and endured the hostility from people on both sides.

One time the fake Chiang Da applied for a temporary job in a food factory and was asked his address, he said, "Treasure Hill".

"What is Treasure Hill? Which street are you living in?"

"There is no street, just a hill."

Treasure hill was an unpermitted settlement built when those low rank soldiers arrived in Taiwan and were not given places to live. That was the place the real Chiang Da told the fake Chiang Da where he could find a place after his release. Fake Chiang Da couldn't mix with those veterans in case people knowing the real Chiang Da would expose him. He shared a place at the edge of the settlement with two Indonesian men because they wouldn't suspect his roots by his accent.

"No address, then how can we mail you the notice?" The interviewer of the food factory said.

"Just put my name and Treasure Hill, people in the community will pass it to me."

Of course he was not hired. People without an address wouldn't be taken as employable. Perhaps he just had to make up an address? Copying an address of an empty house, and if any notice was mailed, he'd break open its mailbox.

"Even Taiwanese pigs have addresses." That's the kind of thing mainlander haters said to express their contempt for homeless retired soldiers. When Taiwan was ruled by the Japanese government, each pig was required to register through its owner with the address of the pigsty. The fake Chiang Da was shocked hearing such obnoxious comments. His family also raised pigs, and he never thought of comparing people to pigs. He was still the same person he had been, but with a different identity. How could he be deemed lower than a pig? In the real Chiang Da's shoes, the fake Chiang Da knew how it felt to be an exiled Chinese, a homeless person completely forgotten by the government he had pledged his loyalty to. Would their status be changed if Taiwan was independent from China?

From time to time, the fake Chiang Da felt the same depression as the late Chiang Da and wished to take his own life. But he couldn't, his life was borrowed. His identity, no matter how lowly it was regarded by others, came at the price of another man's life.

Dear Louise, by switching the identities of two men from opposite political standings, you have successfully presented the plight of each side. In an era in which the misunderstanding of local Taiwanese who are repressed and Mainlanders who suffer from the diaspora become worse over time because of conflicting ideologies and political exploitation, your arrangement provides an opportunity for people to think from the opposite perspective.

As a former political prisoner myself, I know switching identities between inmates was quite unlikely. It is a fictitious story to begin with though, so I congratulate you on your achievement even if it was a stolen story. I wish you a successful literary career, but with your own scenarios from now on.

Yours,
San-Jih

The Undying Tongue of Flame

When Paiz turned seven, she finally was able to go to school with her older brother Fa'ei. Paiz was excited, she had been waiting for this day for a long long time, probably two years, since her brother Fa'ei started going to school.

It took them nearly one-hour to walk from their home to school, and in the winter morning, it could be really cold walking in the windy mountains. Paiz had sensed Fa'ei's reluctance to go to school from time to time, and she made up her mind that she would never be like her brother, she'd be a good student.

It was September, the weather was perfect to walk in the morning. Their parents had prepared lunch for them, sticky rice taro wrapped in lily leaves. Although often it would be cold during the lunch break, it was still the best time of the day in school. Paiz carefully put her lunch in a ramie bag in case it stained her books. She had been given a book of "National Language" and a book of "Common Knowledge". She would have "Advanced National Language", "History" and "Geography" four years later, when she became a fifth grader.

"micu bɨvnɨ si 'ume",
"Plum flowers have blossomed",
"tec'u pesusucaefi 'e mo cono tonsoha.",
"A year is ending." Paiz sang on her walk light-heartedly.

"miko ɨm'ɨmnɨ", seeing a man from their neighborhood, Paiz greeted him happily, "I am going to school!" The man returned her greeting, "huvahi'sio, Goodbye".

Fa'ei was impatient, "ake'i amayahe ho miko coeconɨ, Hurry up."

Then Fa'ei suddenly thought of something and stopped, he spoke to his little sister with a grave tone, "Never use our tribal language in school! Never! You will be punished if you speak our language in school."

Paiz was surprised, she knew they were supposed to learn the "National Language", but she had no idea that the language they used at home was banned in school.

"Is Japanese OK?" She asked cautiously.

"No Japanese, no Taiwanese, only National Language." Fa'ei told her with an expression as cold as snow. Paiz wondered why, but Fa'ei's face frightened her. Maybe she would find out later, after she started classes in school.

In fact, it was very confusing for Paiz to discern these languages from one another. The language they spoke at home was her first language, her mother tongue. Her parents also used it with their relatives and neighbors. But in larger events, like tribesmen's meetings, they'd speak Japanese because they were watched by Japanese police. Of course they could pass on secret messages with their own language in private, and it was exactly the reason why the Japanese rulers prohibited their tribal language. For little Paiz, the language spoken secretly with a very low voice between relatives was their own language, and the language spoken to the officers was Japanese. Not until the end of the war, did Paiz hear the "National Language" for the first time. It was not the Taiwanese she ever heard from people living on the plains, but they seemed to be related. Paiz was told that Taiwanese was a dialect of the "National Language", which was the formal language in China. Paiz did not understand why the "nation" referred to by the adults changed from Japan to China after the war. What really happened during the war? The "National Language" must be quite forceful, because it kicked out the Japanese language—since it came, Japanese was no longer allowed to be used.

In a very short time, Paiz realized why Fa'ei hated school, because students were told to report their classmates who spoke in any language other than the "National Language". Many students were reported, and the punishments could be standing in a corner, or wearing a sign board "I Won't Speak Dialect Again" hung from the offender's chest. And to Fa'ei and Paiz, it was very difficult to communicate in the "National Language" exclusively, since they had just started learning it. Each of them could be reported several times a day for speaking the "primitive language",

Paiz felt that the only thing they did in school was get punished again and again.

Later Paiz realized that, in order not to be punished so many times, the best way was to report others. She became very alert to what language her classmates were speaking, and whenever she caught anyone using Japanese or Taiwanese, she ran to the teachers to report them. It was a very tiring thing to do, because she needed to pay attention to the talking of everyone around her. And, the mutual trust between children was completely destroyed, everyone could be reported by anyone, every child was surrounded by her or his potential enemies.

Paiz's hatred for the "National Language" surged day by day, and writing it was such a touture. There were no written words in their tribal language at all, they memorized things by singing like:

maitan'e nouteuyunu acʉhʉ kokaekaebʉ
All are happy to get together today

teto'sola bumemealʉ 'ananasi'anane o---
We should be cautious, it is our principal

'ananasi'anane ine noana'o acɨhɨ bitotonɨ
Since long time ago, we all worked hard

eto'sola momaemaezo 'ananasi'anane o---
We must learn, it is our principal

And even compared to Japanese, each character of the "National Language" had a lot more strokes. Each day they needed to learn at least five characters, and practice writing each character ten times. By the time Paiz finished her writing, the night had already fallen, and she couldn't go fishing with her dad or help her mom with the weaving, She didn't even have time to hang out with her cousins. Moreover, the characters and their pronunciation seemed to be changing all the time, Paiz never could identify them and how each of them was read, it was so frustrating. She had no doubt that the "National Language" was a monster.

By the end of the semester, when the winter break for the Chinese New Year was near, Paiz had observed something in her school. There were a group of kids speaking the "National Language" fluently because their parents were from China, and the "National Language" was equal to "Chinese". And there was a group speaking Taiwanese, they were mostly from the plains and their ancestors came to Taiwan a long time ago, so they spoke the dialect of the Chinese language, which shared many characters of the "National Language". So kids from the first group would never be punished since the "National Language" was the only language they spoke. And kids from the second groups would be punished from time to time when Taiwanese slipped out of their mouths. As to Paiz and her brother, they were the most frail group since they had to learn Chinese from scratch. In writing, they got confused between Japanese characters and Chinese characters, and in conversations they got confused between their Tsou Language, Japanese and Chinese.

For kids from the Taiwanese group, they had three choices to dodge punishment: First, never making mistakes; second, reporting other kids of their group; third, reporting kids from indigenous communities like Fa'ei and Paiz. And of course the third choice was the easiest, for it was very difficult not to make mistakes at all, and it created enemies in one's own circle by reporting your pals. Thus kids from the indigenous communities became their easiest victims, they were the subalterns of the 3-tiered society formed between the kids. Vaguely, Paiz knew the only strategy for her and her indegious pals to protect themselves was to find and harvest discord among the kids in the second group, so she maintained a distant friendship with kids from the first group. Having peace with the first group was a way to earn respect from the second group, lest they assumed the ethnic Tsou kids were their easy prey.

Once a strategy had been formulated in the mind of Paiz, she felt much more hopeful. Paiz closely observed the kids from the second group, and there was a girl, Lin Ya-Chun, Paiz couldn't judge whether she belonged to the first or the second group. Lin Ya-Chun seemed to speak fluent Chinese, so in the beginning Paiz assumed she was a member of the first group, but she also noticed that Lin Ya-Chun seldom hung out with the members of the first group, and she maintained a distance with members of the second group. Lin Ya-Chun had a follower, Huang Ju-Yao, who was obviously belonging to the second group, and she was Paiz's problem.

Paiz would be reported speaking dialect two or three times a week by Huang Ju-Yao, and at first Paiz thought she could pay attention to Huang Ju-Yao and catch her whenever Taiwanese words came out of her mouth, but it was easier to just avoid Huang Ju-Yao as much as possible. Maintaining a distance from Huang Ju-Yao, Paiz observed that many of Huang Ju-Yao's actions were actually based on Lin Ya-Chun's ideas, she was like Huang Ju-Yao's boss. Additionally, Paiz suspected that Lin Ya-Chun wished to join girls from the first group by having her sidekick Huang Ju-Yao run errands for them, including reporting other kids they did not like. Like Chan Hao, a motherless boy who sometimes smelled oddly and often forgot to bring his handkerchief required by the school's hygiene rule.

Paiz also did not like Chan Hao, but she resented the way he was treated by other kids. She felt so sick that in the school, people picked up each other's problems and made them suffer even more; that was quite contrary to her own community where people solved problems together.

Paiz began to look forward to weekends, so she could have a break from the energy consuming struggles the school gave her. One Sunday, Priest

Frank from the Catholic church of their area took children of Paiz's community for an outing. The programs arranged by Father Frank were the events Paiz loved most. Father Frank was a very old man, older than Paiz's parents. He was from Germany and was assigned to Asia when he was very young. After the war, Father Frank was transferred to Taiwan from the Philippines and started serving in the mountain areas. Father Frank would take kids out at least one Sunday a month for the Sunday School. He taught them Bible reading and at the same time learned things in the wilderness from these children.

This day Paiz and Fa'ei, among other seven or eight children or teenagers of their community and neighboring communities, set out toward the railway station. Father Frank had engaged someone working for the Taiwan Railway Company to introduce them to the topic of how trains worked. Paiz was so excited, she had been waiting for this day for weeks, and the night before she hardly slept, under the feohʉ/moon, she prayed for the daylight to brighten the sky as soon as possible.

When they arrived at the railway station after a

long walk, there were already some other groups waiting for the guided tour around the station. The station was a huge building, probably bigger than the entire area of Paiz's community. Different shapes of wood were nailed or piled or fixed together to be a gigantic structure, compared to the simply built bamboo house of their home, Paiz was amazed. The guide, Mr. Liu introduced that the Alishan forest railway system was one of the few mountain railway systems all over the world. The narrow-gauge railway system was constructed in the 1910s by the Japanese government, for the purpose of logging and timber transport. The highest quality redwood was transported to Japan for the constructions of shrines. The Fenchihu Station they were facing now was where the train met up and exchanged their steam locomotives. Paiz kept hearing the word "modernization", but she did not understand what it meant.

Paiz noticed that Lin Ya-Chun was in the audience, too. She involuntarily lowered her head in case Lin Ya-Chun saw her. During the rest of the tour, Paiz had problems concentrating on Mr. Liu's speech because she tried hard to avoid being noticed by Lin Ya-Chun. Paiz was doing fine hiding herself had she not needed to go to the restroom after the tour was over. It was a long walk back to their community, all children were advised by Father Frank to use the restroom first. When Paiz rushed out of the station restrooms, she bumped into Lin Ya-Chun, who was talking to her sister. Paiz's expression betrayed her surprise and regret, but only for a momentary flash. She quickly got out of the restroom and joined her group. Before taking off, Paiz couldn't help but take a glance at Lin Ya-Chun, who looked distressed.

The following weeks Paiz and her brother's days in school were much more uneventful. The reports of their speaking tribal language reduced significantly. Being left alone, Paiz was able to learn the "National Language" little by little in a more peaceful atmosphere.

Decades later, when Paiz recalled these days, she figured out what really happened and why her fate in school had suddenly changed. Even in the small world of young kids, a hierarchy had formed between students once they figured out each kid's background. There would be some attempting to climb up the social ladder by making friends from the higher tier, it was the case of Huang Ju-Yao and Lin Ya-Chun. Lin Ya-Chun knew speaking perfect Chinese would make her a member of the group of children from the most prestigious class. To achieve that, she would also need to leave her original identity behind, which was that of a Taiwanese speaker. When Paiz ran into her around the Fenchihu Railway Station, she was talking to her sister in her mother tongue, Taiwanese, and she felt that Paiz had found out her secret. To appease Paiz, Lin Ya-Chun stopped bothering her in school in case her unwanted real identity was disclosed by Paiz.

Thinking of this, Paiz laughed bitterly. At that time she only spoke her tribal language and Japanese, she hardly knew Taiwanese from Chinese. But Lin Ya-Chun, being eager to break away from her Taiwanese identity, assumed Paiz had busted her and certainly would blackmail her in school. Paiz had no contact with neither Lin Ya-Chun nor Huang Ju-Yao after school, they belonged to different societies any-way. Where did they end up? How were they doing now? At that time, Lin Ya-Chun must have believed that Paiz's silence about her true identity came from her successful appeasement, because she imagined Paiz was as sophisticated and calculating as she was. But

Paiz wasn't, she wasn't a sophisticated child at all, and wasn't even sophisticated as an adult. Her learning path for mastering "National Language" was challenging, but it indeed opened her view to a world different to her tribal community, the sound, the logic, and the expressions carried by it were so rigorous and precise, she appreciated it very deeply. But thanks to her ancestors, Paiz probably was too "primitive" and naive to feel ashamed of her mother tongue when she was little, which she knew she could have lost completely as she grew older.

Many things had happened to Tsou people during these decades; forced assimilation, cruel oppression of her tribal people's resistance against relocation, bloody deprivation of their traditional territories, and relentless development of their forests. It was a miracle that the Tsou society did not fall apart after all the tragedies they had been through. Paiz knew it was the grand perspective and undefeatable wisdom in her ancestors' language, the undying tongue of flame passed on from generation to generation that gave them hope and strength.

What languages did her classmates speak now?

Had they learned the lessons of any tongue at all? Being a Tsou speaker, Paiz knew she was protected and blessed, and she wished the others would see the significance to her and her people.

Interview by Filip Noubel

Originally published by Asymptote, Jul/04/2019

Filip Noubel (FN): Today Taiwan is one of the freest societies in Asia, yet martial law only ended in 1987, almost forty years after it was first imposed. This period, known as the White Terror, witnessed tremendous political violence: over one hundred and fifty thousand people, including many intellectuals, were arrested, and several thousands were executed. It is also the theme of your previous collection of short stories called *Impossible to Swallow*. What has led you to find inspiration in this particular period of Taiwan's history?

C.J. Anderson-Wu (C.J. A-W): There are several causes, but one of them is my sense of guilt. I did not understand it until I had written several stories. After the Formorsa Incident in 1979, posters of the so-called rebels were everywhere. I was a kid and really believed that they were bad people, that they should be arrested and put in jail. Years went by and as more historical materials were released after the abolishment of martial law, I gradually realized what lies we had lived in. I feel so grateful to those who never backed down and sacrificed so much for the freedom we are enjoying today, and resent my gullibility.

Another thing is that we never had transitional justice. We never had a Nuremberg Trial-type that conducted thorough investigation on what had really happened, why it happened, and who should be responsible. Thus we don't know how we can prevent it from happening again. Today the past dictators are still worshipped, the days under authoritarian rules are still commemorated, and lies are still believed. I was shocked, in despair, and infuriated. How can people stay ignorant when all the evidence is presented in front of their eyes? How can people feel okay sacrificing the rights that were earned by blood, tears, and sweat?

It dawned on me that, no matter how odd it sounds, oppressive power is beguiling to the public; it vibrates with the mystery of human nature. Identifying with it gives people the illusion of power sharing, which is a privilege that belongs only to victors. In other words, the collective denial of victimhood is the reason why dictatorship lasts, the far-right exists, and inequality prevails.

Nevertheless, in literary works, we still find courageous resistance, understandable cowardice, admirable altruism, unavoidable selfishness, unspeakable shame, and familiar fears. When threatened, deprived, hurt, or abused, what choices will we make? When witnessing others being threatened, deprived, hurt, or abused, what actions will we take? When our beloved are threatened, deprived, hurt, or abused, what mind-set will we formulate? Literature is to deal with such dilemmas from different approaches and creative strategies.

Because of the censorship throughout the period of Martial Law, there is a missing part in the spectrum of contemporary Taiwanese literature. It is so incomplete that it is almost impossible to specify what is missing, but the missing part does shape the landscape of recent Taiwanese literature. Are we making it up in the post-Martial Law era? Or have we left it behind? Neither question makes sense. Are we interpreting and reinterpreting it? I have no answer. I looked at the gigantic blankness for a while, and decided that the contour of this blankness is the White Terror.

FN: Your work lies at the crossroad of fiction and non-fiction as you often mention historical events. Most short stories sound like testimonies of that period. It also reminds me of the 傷痕文學, the Scar Literature of China in the 1970s, that depicts the atrocities committed against intellectuals during Mao's Cultural Revolution. The issues of loyalty, courage, but also betrayal and denial dominate your prose as they show the internal struggles your characters go through. Do you agree then that "fiction is more real than truth"?

C.J. A-W: Yes, fiction is the only path toward the truths that we are still unable to confront directly. "Scar Literature" is a good term, as we are left with so many scars from that history, and many of them are still unhealed. Ironically, in the 1970s and 1980s, Taiwan used a lot of Scar Literature in China for anti-communist propaganda in order to justify the tightening control on thought in Taiwan. Looking back, we probably can conclude that anti-communism propaganda at that time did not work at all, considering how many Taiwanese people today are embracing the commercial interests in China rather than the freedom of speech. It was oppression in the name of anti-communism, and people were conditioned by the terrible rules in Taiwan during the Martial Law era, not because they were really convinced that the Chinese communist regime was evil. The consequence is, since we have more of an open attitude toward Marxism and communism today, we don't see the evil of dictatorship because our own society was also shaped by dictatorship.

We are so used to being taught what to do and what to follow. And when doubts were raised by the few dissidents, not only did the rulers feel disturbed, but the mainstream population did as well. One needs to be very brave to stand up against injustice, for her/his voices might be muffled, and her/his activism might be blocked by people close to her/him. Repression is more common than we could have imagined, especially when we fail to learn the lessons from the past. Given how screwed-up world politics is nowadays, I have to re-disclose old scars in my writing. I have problems staying silent while foreseeing new infections spreading over old wounds.

FN: Taiwanese society has evolved from a narrow narrative dominated by Kuomintang ideology to a much more diverse identity embracing and mixing the cultures of the native peoples, of the first Chinese settlers usually referred to as Taiwanese, and of the mainlanders from China who migrated massively after 1949. To this one can add the influence of fifty years of Japanese occupation and the recent trends in globalization. In this incredible mix, and at a time when some actors and survivors of the White Terror are still alive, has there been a conscious effort to face the painful past, to discuss it publicly? Has it succeeded, in your opinion? Has art played a major role in it?

C.J. A-W: Japan did kick off the modernization of Taiwan with a very solid infrastructure, but the political oppression was no less brutal. And as the Nationalist Party (Kuomintang) was taking over Taiwan, the bloody 228 Incident which killed thousands of elites cultivated by the Japanese education system and the following period of White Terror made many local Taiwanese people think Japan was a better ruler. Therefore right after the 228 Incident, the Japanese language was banned along with all Japanese publications, and Taiwanese dialect was strictly limited. To strengthen the patriotism of the "Republic of China," the government in exile encouraged anti-colonialist literature. For decades, stories (fictional and non-fictional) of insurgencies during the Japanese colonialist era were relatively abundant, for they happened to serve the ideology of the Nationalist Party at that time. Naturally, seeds of resistance against authoritarianism were secretly carried in these stories.

With such an intertwined history and without any legal procedure regarding transitional justice, it is almost impossible to comb through the past and come up with a historical narrative that is widely agreed upon. Furthermore, up until today, there are still secret documents of past injustices that remain unreleased, further complicating our establishment of any historical perspective. And, to our regret, the tremendous fear and shame still stop many victims from telling their own stories. That's why the role of art is so crucial. The victims of White Terror included not only those who were directly persecuted but also their families, as exemplified by many characters in my stories, as well as in the stories in other Taiwanese works of literature. Imagine a victim who has remained silent for decades reading a story comparable to her/his experience, how relieved she/he might feel by knowing that she/he is not alone and what had happened was not her/his fault.

FN: Why did you decide to opt for English to write this collection of short stories?

C.J. A-W: English is my father language, ha ha. When I was in my early thirties I often, in my restless sleep and dreams, used English to quarrel with my father. I realized that was how I defied patriarchal social norms, and English made me more audacious. My father was a judge in Taiwan Apellate Court, "Judge Not" was my first short story; with the character of a judge, I revisited the delicate situation my father could have been through. Although it was written years after my father's passing, I felt closer to him and was able to understand him more deeply.

Another reason to use English is, after publishing Chung Wenyin's *Decayed Land* (translated by Dr. Pao-Fang Hsu), several readers kindly told me that while they had tried, it was too difficult for them to read the history of a Taiwanese family that was shaken by the White Terror. So *Impossible to Swallow* was

186

my attempt to communicate with readers who didn't have any knowledge about White Terror in Taiwan. Taiwan is so marginalized in the global readership, and the translation and promotion of Taiwanese literature are so slow and ineffective. I hope my works will catalyze the interactions between Taiwanese writers and readers of international literature.

FN: You are yourself a publisher. How difficult is it to maintain this career in Taiwan? Is there a significant support from readers, bookstores, or the government to sustain small independent publishing houses? What is the reading culture in Taiwan today?

C.J. A-W: There are grants and awards for publishing literature, but still it is quite tough to survive. Debates over Fixed Book Price (FBP) as a policy to support small publishers and bookstores have been undergoing for a long time, but no conclusion has ever been reached. Publishers can apply for grants to translate and publish Taiwanese literature, but it is very competitive.

Crowd funding for individual publishing is a trend, but can be tricky. Independent bookstores can also apply for grants to support their events, such as writers' reading, speeches, or panels. From time to time there are bookstores going out of business, but also, on the other hand, there are new bookstores setting up. Independent bookstores are trying all kinds of strategies to sustain themselves, like selling drinks and light meals, or even selling fresh vegetables directly provided by farmers.

Although the sales of books keep declining, I don't think it is because reading is in decline. We read a lot online, which certainly has reduced the need to buy books. As for literature, it is naturally more and more challenging for contemporary writers to sell their works, because all the classics and masterpieces are still on the market. For example, when my books are to be presented in bookstores, they will be placed next to Isaac Asimov, Margaret Atwood, and Ivo Andri, among other established authors whose last names start with A. I'd kiss anyone who notices my works at all. Nevertheless, writing, and reading literature are still big in Taiwan, through diversified mediums, including paperbacks, eBooks, and online platforms. In Taiwan, audiobooks are developing relatively slowly.

FN: You also work as a literary translator? What are the main authors, languages and countries that usually get translated in Taiwan?

C.J. A-W: Yes, I translated William Golding's *Darkness Visible* into Chinese, it was my favorite work of translation. Later on I worked with English-speaking editors in translating Taiwanese literature into English. Currently I am translating Yang Chingchu's *Blackfoot Village.*

Taiwan is a huge literature importer. Japanese literature must be number one in readers' minds, Haruki Murakami's popularity is unparalleled, and Japanese master writers like Osamu Dazai, among others, are still printed and reprinted.

English is the dominant language in translated literature here and everywhere; literary works from the US, UK, Australia are the most common, and some are from Canada, Ireland, and New Zealand. Award-winning works are more likely to be published in Chinese. Nobel Prize winners, Man Booker winners and Pulitzer winners usually will be introduced to Taiwanese readers. And if translated works from

Indian or Sri Lankan writers, like Arundhati Roy and Michael Ondaatje, are available, it is because they have won big literary prizes or have been made into movies. I'd like to see more South African literature in Taiwan, but except for J.M. Coetzee, there are few—even Nadine Gordimer's works are not familiar to Taiwanese readers.

Chinese versions of European literature are still few, too few, and literary works of original languages other than Spanish, French, and German are hardly found. Korean literature is a growing category in bookstores these days, thanks to grants from the Korean government. The New Southbound Policy, originally a policy of the Tsai Administration to distract businesses from overly relying on China, has begun bringing in Southeast Asian literature to Taiwan, I expect to see it blooming.

C.J. Anderson-Wu published *Impossible to Swallow—a Collection of Short Stories about White Terror in Taiwan* in 2017. Her short stories have appeared in the Anthology of Short Stories in English, Eastlit, Lunaris Review, and Strands Lit, Short Story Avenue, Short Story Town, Kitaab, among other literary journals. She has translated several significant literary works Such as *Darkness Visible* by British writer William Golding, *Fanny: Being the True History of the Adventures of Fanny Hackabout-Jones* by American writer Erica Jong, and *Decayed Lust* by Taiwanese writer Chung Wenyin, among others. Since 2006, her priority has been to build up an international readership for Taiwanese literature.

Filip Noubel was born in a Czech-French family, and raised in Tashkent and Athens. He studied Slavonic and East Asian languages in Tokyo, Paris, Prague, and Beijing. He now pursues a double career as a journalist and literary translator. After ten years in Beijing, he now works as Managing Editor for Global Voices Online, a citizen journalism platform that publishes in over 40 languages. He has translated and published a number of Czech, Chinese, Tibetan, and Uzbek authors in French, and serves as Editor-at-Large for Central Asia at Asymptote Journal. He currently spends his time between Prague, Tbilisi, Tashkent, and Taipei.

The Surveillance

Author: C. J. Anderson-Wu

Publisher: Kanda Yasuko Memorial Foundation

Editors: Steven M. Anderson, Ginny Jaramillo

Designer: Chung Pei-Ying

Date of Publication: Oct/01/2021

Prices: 11.99USD, 300NTD

ISBN: 978-957-43-8907-0

Special thanks to the cover artist: Rudou Lin
Age of Ambition: The Ocean at the End (2015)